Praise for
A STELLAR PURPOSE

"Natacha tells a beautiful narrative of what might be possible for humanity. But is it only a story? This full book will make you wonder about your own potential."

—Jim Self, Mastering Alchemy

"A timely, unique, and creative story that Belair accomplishes with grace and originality."

—Emily Keefer, Author of *The Stars on Vita Felice Court*

"A parallel universe as one storyline and an important social message as another. *A Stellar Purpose* is stellar indeed. This book surpasses parameters such as target audiences and age groups. It is one and all. It tells a story with a purpose, giving readers one in exchange. Maybe, from Avery's story, we will be inspired to take care of the planet that provides for us."

—Grace Jackson, Book Critic

"Natacha Belair presents a unique coming-of-age novel in which the protagonist struggles to accomplish her life's true purpose. This fascinating tale, filled with thought-provoking ideas, will inspire you to take your future into your own hands, and embrace the abundance of joy, peace, and freedom that life has to offer."

—Dr. Scott Zarcinas, Founder and Director, 818: Unlocking Your Life

"This book is more than fiction. It is a story about courage and faith—the courage to embrace and stay true to who we truly are and the faith that we, no matter who we are, can make a difference if we believe we can. Through her fantastic adventure, Avery teaches us that our collective future can be amazing. It really is up to every single one of us!"

—Nathalie Arseneault, Organic Foodie, Local TV Host

"A book intended for adolescents that adults will love too—and learn from. It is a fast-paced, transformative story about personal growth that will make you think twice about how you see the world."

—Wally Jones, Multi-Award-Winning Author of *Sam the Chosen*

"I loved it! Mrs. Belair explores some of the realities found in the fifth dimension and touches upon important environmental topics in a riveting and forward-thinking story that keeps you on the edge of your seat until the very last page."

—Léandre Audet, Reiki Master, Mastering Alchemy Graduate

"As you are transported into Avery's alternate dimension, the author uses her extraordinary creation of imagination and allows the readers to totally immerse themselves in this clever story with her beautifully crafted, descriptive prose. Avery and her friends set out to save the De La Grotta Zoo after they skillfully discover the malfeasance that is going on in there. Mrs. Belair takes you on a journey that does not disappoint."

—Bill Sheehan, Award-Winning Author of *A Tail Among Tales*

"This story will appeal to both the young and the young at heart. Natacha Belair takes us on a journey through parallel universes and great emotions. Readers will become more mindful of humanity's fate and will want to better themselves so they may have a positive impact on our wonderful planet."

—Manon Côté, Writer, Editor, Book Critic

A Stellar Purpose

By Natacha Belair

ISBN 978-1-64663-781-2

Website: NatachaBelair.com
Illustrations: Natacha Belair

OCEANSTORM PUBLISHING
Sparking Imagination. Inspiring Change.

Ottawa, Ontario, Canada

A STELLAR PURPOSE

NATACHA BELAIR

OTTAWA
ONTARIO, CANADA

Dedications

To my parents—without whom this story would not exist.
To my two very best friends—for their ongoing support and insight.
To my two loving daughters—for believing in my dream, and never doubting it would actually come true.
To my beloved husband—who always points me in the right direction, and to whom I gladly bestow the title of plot co-creator.
Thank you.

Author's Note

I wrote *A Stellar Purpose* to . . .

Invite people of all ages to realize their ultimate potential.

Entice human beings to treat each other and their surroundings with respect.

Inspire this generation—which is filled with passionate people eager to do their part to help save the planet—to come up with innovative ways to fix the mistakes of those who lived on Earth before them.

I hope you will join me in doing all you can to ensure our beautiful world thrives for millennia to come.

—*Natacha*

CHAPTER 1

IDEAS, FACTS, REVELATIONS . . . Avery wakes with a pounding heart. She reaches for Daisy, gently patting the older of her two dogs to soothe herself as she attempts to unriddle the remarkable dream she just had.

As she lies in the darkness, a warm, tingling sensation begins to spread throughout her body. Looking down, she sees that she is glowing. Hypnotized by the dancing blue lights, Avery's subconscious is gently pulled into another dimension. She finds herself standing on a strange red planet, with clusters of colourful clouds laid over black, endless space, speckled with millions of white stars and distant planets.

As if from nowhere, a tall, handsome being appears next to her. Avery stares into his gorgeous, emerald-green eyes before turning her attention to his thick, wavy, forest-green hair that magically falls perfectly back into place as he runs his fingers through it. Dressed in varying shades of green, he wears a slim-fit blazer, dress shirt, and tapered pants. He extends a hand and Avery accepts, curling her fingers around his. As they touch, she feels her body morph.

"Whoa . . . what was that?"

"Welcome, Avery."

"You know my name?"

"Yes, I do. Let me help you see what your inner being looks like."

My inner being?

The stylish entity waves his left hand, and a full-length mirror appears. Avery's stunned to see an elegant being clothed in an exquisite, one-shoulder dress gazing back at her.

"What's up with this mirror? That's not me. The girl in the reflection is way older than I am, and she looks like a movie star."

"Take your time. Have another look. I know this is hard to believe, but there's nothing wrong with the mirror. This is what your inner being looks like. This is the 'real' you."

Puzzled, Avery moves closer to the mirror, staring into her teal-blue eyes. *This can't be me. I look like I'm at least twenty years old!* She backs up as her long, dark auburn hair and royal-blue gown sway easily with every movement.

"What's happening? Who are you? Where am I?"

"My name is Zander. I know this is unexpected, but please believe me, there's nothing to fear. I'm here to introduce you to your life's true purpose."

"What are you talking about? My dreams tonight are completely nuts. I must have eaten too many cookies before bed or something."

"Haha! Kamila told me you had a funny sense of humour."

"Kamila? You know my grandma?"

"I do know your grandmother."

"What do you mean, 'do'? She died when I was little."

"Yes, this is true. But now, she lives here with us."

"May I see her?"

"Not today, but soon. I promise," Zander sees the disappointment in Avery's eyes. Trying to bring back the focus of the conversation, he asks, "Have you ever noticed that you have a special connection with animals?"

"Well . . . I've always had a lot of pets, and I volunteer at the zoo."

"Yes, but more than that. From what I've heard, you've only been on

Earth for fifteen years, and you've already saved several creatures."

"Oh yeah . . . like last year, when my sister and I helped that baby duck."

"You rescued a duckling?"

"Yes, and it was really sad at first, actually."

"Really? What happened?"

"So, each spring, my grandfather raises ducks to control the weeds that grow in the pond in his front yard. One day, when my sister and I went to see the new babies, we noticed that one had been rejected by his mother and was being bullied by his brothers and sisters. We took care of the poor little thing until he was strong enough to fend for himself. And it worked! When we took him back to the nest, his mother and siblings greeted him with open wings."

"Haha! I'm definitely going to enjoy getting to know you."

"You will?"

"Yes, you'll be visiting this place a lot over the coming months. Discovering your life's purpose doesn't happen overnight."

"My life's purpose?"

Zander offers a reassuring smile. "As I was saying a few minutes ago, you may not realize it, but you have an innate connection with animals. This is because you're an animal protector."

"I'm a what now?"

"An animal protector. This is your life's mission. You must find ways to watch over animals and help the planet flourish."

"What? None of this makes any sense. How am I supposed to do that?"

"Don't worry. You're not alone. We'll help you deal with this new reality as it unfolds."

"Yeah . . . but . . ."

"It'll be okay, Avery. Trust me." Zander smiles softly, before disappearing as suddenly as he arrived.

CHAPTER 2

THE NEXT MORNING, Avery wakes up with two snoozing dogs on her bed.

"I love you guys. Come here, Lexie. Come on," whispers Avery, gently play fighting with the younger of her two dogs. Her three pets bring so much joy to her family's household—and this morning, she feels even closer to them.

Smiling ear to ear, she slips out of bed and tiptoes to the bathroom, almost tripping over her cat, Shadow. She gently picks up the fattest of her pets, kissing him good morning and giving him an extra long cuddle. As she buries her face in his deep black fur, she starts to sense blue heat radiating from her body—the same feeling she had last night.

As she reaches the bathroom, Avery sighs loudly.

Of course.

Teagan, Avery's younger sister, is always a few minutes quicker than she is to get up and jump in the shower. Sitting on the floor next to the bathroom door, with Shadow purring happily on her lap, she relives every minute of last night's adventure. Suddenly feeling completely overwhelmed, Avery stops petting Shadow and begins to bite her nails.

How can I concentrate on school? Or exams. Or anything, really. What am I supposed to do with all of this? I can't tell anyone. They'll think I'm bonkers!

Avery quickly snaps back to reality as the bathroom door swings open and Teagan waltzes out with her steamed-up glasses and her long, curly, strawberry-blond hair dripping all over her school uniform.

"All yours, Ave." Teagan smiles, before her eyebrows furrow with concern. "Are you okay?"

Avery bites at her nails again while trying to come up with a white lie. "I guess I'm nervous about my test."

"Chill out. You always freak out for nothing. You know you'll do okay."

Avery rolls her eyes and sighs as Teagan walks away, with Shadow following in her wake.

Teag's right. I do need to chill out.

She gets to her feet and walks into the bathroom, wiping the steam from the mirror with her hand and frowning at her reflection, no longer seeing any trace of her inner being, but just the familiar brown shoulder-length hair and grey-blue eyes. For a moment, she feels normal—like she did before last night.

After washing and quickly putting on one of her favourite outfits—a pair of loose-fitting, light-coloured jeans and a bright-purple, long-sleeved T-shirt—Avery makes her way downstairs and grabs some breakfast, before joining Teagan at the kitchen counter. Her sister doesn't bother looking up from her smartphone as she mindlessly shoves a peanut butter and jelly sandwich into her mouth.

Maybe everything's normal. Maybe last night's dreams were just that— really strange dreams. Avery sighs deeply and swirls the spoon around in her oatmeal.

Her thoughts are interrupted by her mother. "Do you girls want a ride to school this morning? You're running a bit behind."

Teagan nods enthusiastically, her mouth too full of PB & J to reply.

Avery smiles weakly. "Thanks, Mom, but I'll walk. I want to get some fresh air before my history test."

She hugs her mother, Isabel, and gives her stepfather, Eric, a kiss on the forehead—something she started ten years ago when they first met—and gives Teagan a light, sisterly punch on the arm before heading out the door to make her way to school.

CHAPTER 3

ALTHOUGH SHE'S RUNNING LATE, Avery walks slowly, lost in her thoughts, until she's startled back into the present by the feeling of warm hands pressed over her eyes.

"Guess who?" A familiar voice laughs.

"Yuk, Page! Your hands are all sweaty." Avery grabs her friend's wrists and pulls her hands away from her face. Paige laughs again and wipes her fingers on Avery's top.

"What's up with you? I called your name like three times."

"Did you? Sorry. I guess I was daydreaming."

"Oh, yeah? About Jake?"

"Aah, stop it, Paige! I still can't believe he's actually my boyfriend."

"It's pretty amazing, considering how defective you are." Paige laughs. Avery punches her friend lightly on the arm.

"Okay, okay. I was just teasing . . . hey, check this out," Paige pulls off the hood of her crop top grey hoodie to reveal a short, messy hairdo dyed candyfloss pink.

"Seriously?! You chopped it all off! Turn around. Let me see." Avery steers her best friend to see the back of her head. "You look amazing! You're completely nuts. I mean, it looks awesome. I just can't believe you had the guts to do that. I can't even bring myself to let my bangs grow out."

"I can't wait to see what people think." Paige smiles cheekily.

"I'm sure you'll get a ton of compliments," Avery replies, looking proudly at her friend.

Paige shrugs and changes the subject, not wanting to keep the spotlight on herself for too long. "So, are you stressed about the test?"

"A bit, but I think I prepped enough. Fingers crossed. You?"

"You know me. If I pass, I'll be—"

The end of Paige's sentence is cut off as a man screams, "Shelby! Shelby! Come here, Shelby!"

Paige and Avery turn in the direction of the voice and see a Boston Terrier heading straight into traffic.

Avery lifts both hands and shouts, "No, Shelby! Stay!"

The dog stops dead in its tracks, looks at Avery, sits, and stays. As soon as there is a gap in the traffic, Avery crosses the road and grabs the dog's leash as the owner runs up, gasping for air.

"I don't know what happened . . . she never runs away. I don't know how to thank you."

"No worries, mister." Avery hands over the leash. "I'm glad I was able to help." She scooches down and gently pats Shelby's head. "You be careful now." Shelby attentively looks at her new friend as though she can understand every word and gives her a tiny lick on the chin.

"That was intense." Paige whistles softly. "Why does this kind of thing always happen to you? It's as if you're connected to animals or something."

Avery nods slowly, her thoughts turning once again to the strange events of the night before.

CHAPTER 4

LATER THAT DAY, Avery stands at her locker looking at her phone when a voice from behind her sends a tingle through her body.

"Hey, babe. How'd you do on your test?"

She lifts her head, her face flushing with pleasure and nervousness as Jake approaches. "I think I did okay. How was music class?"

"It was awesome!" Jake leans over and kisses her cheek, making her blush even more deeply. "I got behind the kit and totally rocked out!" Avery smiles at the thought that not only is her long-term crush now her real-life boyfriend, but he's also an amazingly cool drummer.

They grab their duffel bags, stuffed with their mandatory green and grey PE gear, and head to gym class. As always, Jake cracks jokes in the hope of seeing Avery's beautiful smile, which is quite easy given she is completely head over heels for him.

As they walk, Avery takes in his muscular shoulders, wrapped tightly in his black T-shirt. As well as being an amazing drummer, Jake is part of the school swim team, and the hours of training show in his gorgeous physique.

How could I land such a jock? Jake's sooo dreamy. I can't believe he actually asked me out last month—

"Babe, are you with me? Are you daydreaming or something?"

"Oh . . . umm . . ." Avery's cheeks flush pink again, feeling awkward for getting caught in a moment of infatuation.

"No worries. I was asking if you saw the video I sent you this morning."

"Umm . . . yeah . . ." Avery answers desperately trying to find her bearings. "That was really cute. The baby goat couldn't stop licking the dog's face."

"It's hard to tell who's enjoying it more, the dog or the goat." They both laugh as they push open the swing doors to the gym.

"Yoga mats," states Avery. "I thought we were playing basketball today."

"Ms. Gupta is so random." Jake shakes his head. They make their way to the back of the room and drop their sweaters onto two mats, to make sure they can be next to each other for the class, before heading to the changing rooms and getting into their shorts and T-shirts.

After twenty minutes of stretching, the class collectively groans when Ms. Gupta asks everyone to lie down on their mats for a calming meditation exercise.

Avery seems to be the only one who is enjoying today's unusual gym class. When she lies down, she hears some of her classmates' whisper and complain about the music and how boring the class is.

Avery looks at Jake and whispers in the softest voice possible, so she doesn't get caught talking, "I like this. It feels nice to take a few minutes to relax and not chase after a ball for an hour."

Jake smiles and whispers back, "You're so weird. That's why I like you so much."

Avery squints and awkwardly smiles back. *What was that about? Jake thinks I'm weird . . . shoot! Why did I say—*

Avery's thoughts are interrupted by Ms. Gupta. "Now that you have stretched your bodies, you will see that this is a wonderful way to stretch your minds. Haha!" Ms. Gupta laughs out loud. Alone. Avery sends her a reassuring smile, feeling bad for her classmates' lack of reaction. "Now, close your eyes and clear your thoughts. Imagine yourself on a beautiful beach. Take several deep breaths of the humid, salty air. You hear gentle waves crashing as you sense the warmth of the sun on your skin. At a distance, you see thick palm trees filled with tiny, yellow birds that chirp beautiful melodies."

Carefully following the instructions, Avery feels an odd resonance in her body. Opening her eyes, she no longer sees her imagined beach but rather our majestic galaxy. Just as she did last night. She has entered the parallel universe once again. She looks down to see long, dark auburn hair covering her shoulders and part of a gorgeous blue gown. It's undeniable—she has morphed into her paranormal state.

Shocked—Avery opens her eyes, sits up, and stares at the sea of green T-shirts and grey shorts—immediately catching Ms. Gupta's attention. Embarrassed, she lays back down and hesitantly closes her eyes.

Lifelike images of the galaxy appear once more as she hears, "Welcome back, Avery." She squeals uncontrollably and hastily sits up.

Confused, nearby students open their eyes to see who is disturbing the class. Although Ms. Gupta is visibly upset, she remains calm and authoritatively whispers, "Stop making noise, Avery. Class—close your eyes and lie still."

Oh, no . . . this is sooo embarrassing. This is the worst thing that has ever happened to me!

Trying to ignore the surrounding giggles, she lies back down and closes her eyes—instantly draping her temples with warm tears.

Ms. Gupta continues with her meditation reading, but there's no use; Avery can't focus. *What's going on? It felt so real. Just like last night.*

She tries to calm herself down, but her breathing becomes quicker and louder. Jake turns his head in her direction and sees that his girlfriend is clearly distressed.

"Babe, what's up?" he whispers. "You look like you're hyperventilating. Do you need to see the school nurse or something?"

She kindly shrugs him off and panthers a white lie. "I think I messed up my history test."

"Chill out. I'm sure you did fine," adds Jake as he closes his eyes.

Avery looks at the oversized gym clock. *Good! Class is almost over. I just want to go home and lie under the covers.* She focuses on the clock. *Only three minutes to go. You can do this, Avery.*

Seconds later, her mind uncontrollably wanders to extraordinary visions of the universe. *What's happening to me? Why can't I get rid of these images?* Frustrated, she takes a deep breath and tries to find answers to some of her million questions. *What's going on? Will this happen every time I try to relax? Or read a book? Or listen to music? What about when I try to fall asleep tonight? Or tomorrow? Or the next day?*

"I can't take this," utters Avery. She stands up and runs from the room, oblivious to Jake and Ms. Gupta calling after her.

CHAPTER 5

AVERY HAS NEVER even pretended to be sick to skip school, so running out of class in the middle of the day is a strange and unfamiliar experience, but there's no way she's going back now. She can't face Jake or the rest of the students. She feels bad knowing that Jake and Paige will be worried about her, but it will be easier to go back after the long weekend and say that she felt ill, rather than having to answer difficult questions now.

She clings onto the silver lining that Monday is a public holiday, and hopes that by Tuesday, everyone will have forgotten what happened in gym class.

The other thing weighing on her mind, as she slowly walks home, is that on Friday afternoons, she volunteers at the De La Grotta Zoo.

Avery loves volunteering at the zoo, and values her friendship with Skyler, her mentor, as much as the relationships she's created with the animals. Skyler's nineteen, but her slight build and the way she treats Avery as an equal makes the younger girl feel as though they are contemporaries, and their shared love of animals has given them a natural closeness.

If Mom finds out that I skipped out of school early, there's no way she'll let me go to the zoo this afternoon, and I'm really looking forward to seeing Kiki and Koko.

Feeling bad about having to lie to her mother, Avery comes up with a plan as she enters the front door of her house.

"Hi, Mom!"

"Ave? What are you doing home so early?"

She nervously replies, "Ms. Gupta decided to give us the afternoon off because she's heading out of town for the long weekend and wanted to beat traffic."

"Lucky you!"

"I know, right?" she replies, feeling both relieved and guilty. She enters her room and feels herself slowly begin to calm down as she relives her first day as a volunteer.

"Good morning, everyone, and welcome to the De La Grotta Zoo family," said Mr. Bravebird, the volunteer coordinator. "Today, you will be matched with a seasoned employee who will teach you everything you need to know in the hope that you will become an official employee one day."

"I'd love that!" exclaimed Avery, who immediately felt embarrassed for the inability to contain her excitement.

Skyler, who loves Avery's enthusiasm, immediately stated, "I'll take her! Well, I mean . . . if that's okay with you, Mr. Bravebird."

"That's a terrific idea, Skyler. This young lady seems to be as keen as you are. So, let's start with you. Please tell us your name and why you decided to become a De La Grotta Zoo volunteer."

Avery, who typically hates being put on the spot, especially to speak in front of others, was eager to share her story. "Hi, my name is Avery Westwater. I'm fifteen years old. I fell in love with this place when my aunt brought me here for my eighth birthday, and I've been looking forward to this day ever since. So, today's the best day of my life!"

"That's wonderful," replied Mr. Bravebird. "No pressure, you guys, but this one's tough to beat. Who wants to go next?"

Neither of the two other newbies spoke up; they knew their story wasn't as compelling as Avery's.

At the end of the thirty-minute welcome session, Skyler gave Avery a tour of the facilities, pointing out every bathroom they encountered.

"Out of everything you'll discover today, this is the most important thing to remember."

"Are you serious? Why?"

"You'll quickly notice that the question you'll be asked the most will be *where's the bathroom?*" She winked and smiled at her new mentee.

CHAPTER 6

LATER THAT AFTERNOON, as Avery enters the zoo's nursing station, Skyler says, "Ave, please grab the two bottles from the fridge and warm them up a bit."

"Okay, I'm on it," she replies, genuinely at ease with the whole process. "I still can't believe I get to hold baby koalas every time I volunteer."

"I feel the same." Skyler reaches into the incubator, gently wraps Kiki in a blanket, and hands her over to Avery. "It's too bad Kuanju can't take care of her two joeys, but at least she's getting stronger every day."

"Yeah, good thing she didn't give birth to twins in the wild. I looked it up online. Koalas almost never have twins." Avery snuggles with Kiki, who closes her eyes and gently holds Avery's face. *You're so soft, baby girl.* Avery inhales deeply as she tickles the baby's belly with her nose.

"That's right," replies Skyler, who heads to the bottle warmer with Koko delicately nestled in her arms. "If Kuanju had given birth in the wild, odds are, all three of them would have died. Especially since both her babies have exceptionally light fur. Can you imagine what a predator would do if it saw two unprotected, white, fluffy fur balls in a tree?"

"Ouch!"

"Exactly!" Skyler reaches for the empty rocking chair beside Avery and starts chatting away.

Avery loves listening to Skyler's stories about the zoo. She always seems to have the latest scoop. As a volunteer, Avery isn't allowed to go into the restricted areas, which include the enclosures with the more dangerous animals, as well as certain parts of the building.

When she first started, Skyler told Avery that the zoo was built on the site of an old industrial warehouse, and that a huge storage area, twice the size of the actual zoo, still existed.

She recently told Avery that since the new owners took over the zoo a few months ago, they got rid of some of the old staff, hired loads of new people, and opened a massive veterinary clinic in the storage area, which she hasn't been able to see because only the new staff are allowed.

Avery asks, "So, have you been able to chat with the new vet staff yet?" She looks at Kiki, who finished her bottle a few minutes ago and dozed off in her arms.

"No, not yet," replies Skyler, tearing up. "Things are so different now. It drives me nuts. I used to be able to hang out with the vets and help them out. It was a great experience for me, and they were happy for the help. Now, none of them even know I'm studying to become a vet myself."

"Why don't you sit next to one of them when you're having lunch and try to make friends?"

"I guess I could try," Skyler says. She places Koko's empty bottle on the table and pulls the blanket over his eyes to help him doze off. He gently wraps his right paw around her thumb. "Hazel seems friendly enough, and she's actually kind of cute. Okay, I'll try that next time we end up in the lunchroom together."

CHAPTER 7

THE NEXT MORNING, Eric packs up the car as the family prepares for the two-hour car ride to spend the long weekend with Isabel's father, Marcus.

Avery climbs into the back seat and closes her eyes, trying to imagine how the house will look now that all the snow has finally melted after the extra long winter. Both Avery and Teagan have always enjoyed visiting their grandparents' home, as there's always lots to do. In the summer, they go for extreme bike rides or climb the rocks in the nature reserves. In the winter, they build snow sculptures and go tobogganing.

The journey goes by quickly, and it feels like only minutes have passed when Avery smiles at the sight of her grandfather standing on the front steps. "Mom, I told you Grandpa would be wearing a blue golf shirt again. You owe me five bucks!"

"Honey, don't laugh at your grandpa. I know it's kind of odd that he owns at least twenty different blue golf shirts, even though he stopped playing golf thirty years ago. But you know how he is. He loves that style, and he wears it well."

"Yeah, yeah. I know, Mom. I was only teasing," Avery replies, rolling her eyes.

The moment the car stops, Avery jumps out, runs up the steps, and leaps into Marcus's arms. Their hug is quickly interrupted by a teenaged, blue-eyed, overly excited Husky. Lexie runs out of the car almost as quickly as Avery did, body-slamming into her favourite grandparent.

"Lexie . . . be careful, girl! Grandpa's getting old!"

"Hey, I'm not that old," Marcus replies, chuckling.

"What are you doing now? Silly girl! Get your big butt off Grandpa's foot."

Lexie immediately stands and leans her heavy front paws on her grandfather, who falls to his knees.

"You missed me. Didn't you, girl? Yes, you did," says Marcus as Lexie repeatedly licks his face.

The day is sunny and warm, with a fresh spring breeze rolling down from the surrounding hills, blowing a hint of spring flowers into the house. As soon as they've unpacked the car, Teagan and Avery rush out into the woods with their young Husky and their old chocolate Labrador, only coming home at dusk. They sit around the campfire eating s'mores and drinking hot coco while their grandfather tells them lovely stories of Grandma Kamila late into the night.

The following morning, Avery makes her way to the kitchen, rubbing the sleep from her eyes.

"Avery, sweetie, you're finally up!" Her grandfather welcomes her with a smile.

"Mmm," she replies happily. "Is it just me, or does it smell like pancakes?"

"It does, but I ate the last one a few minutes ago." Teagan laughs.

"You're kidding, right?" Avery's eyes widen with horror that she might have missed out on her grandfather's pancakes.

"You snooze, you lose." Teagan giggles, darting out of the way before Avery can land a punch on her arm. "Only kidding! There are a few left in the oven."

As Avery and Teagan finish the last few bites of their breakfast, Eric comes in with the morning paper.

"Have you seen the news this morning?" he asks, looking concerned.

"Not yet. Why?" Marcus replies.

"Look. Read this." Eric hands the newspaper to his father-in-law.

"Oh my, this is horrible."

"What is it, Dad? What happened?" asks Isabel.

"There was a chemical spill in Whaleford last night."

"Oh no! Where? Was anyone hurt?" asks Teagan.

"I don't know. Hold on, I'll read the article aloud so everyone can hear the details."

Local man called 9-1-1 on Friday night at 7:53 p.m. to report a strong odour that caused a burning sensation in his lungs and made his wife dizzy and nauseous. The couple's house is located on the river near the De La Grotta Zoo.

"Oh no." Avery can't keep the anxiety out of her voice. "Are the animals okay?"

"They said *near* the zoo. Not *at* the zoo," Marcus reassures her, and then carries on reading.

Nearby residents were forced to leave their homes for three hours while emergency crews tried their best to contain the chemicals that seeped into the river. Police are working to pinpoint the exact chemical composition and establish the possible short-term and long-term effects this incident may have on wildlife and waterways. Firefighters spent the night cleaning up the spill. Despite their efforts, hundreds of fish and close to two-dozen waterbirds were found dead this morning along the riverbank. It is still unknown how many chemicals were dumped and by whom, but police are following a few potential leads.

"That's horrible. All those poor animals. Who would do something like that?" Avery's eyes fill with tears as she thinks about the loss of life.

"I don't know, sweetie. Maybe it was an accident. At least they were able to contain the situation quickly. It could have been a lot worse." Her grandfather gently squeezes her shoulder. "I'm sure it'll be old news by the time you head home tomorrow afternoon. Now then, didn't you want to go for a hike in the woods this morning?"

"Yeah, I did." Avery grabs a napkin and wipes her nose.

"It's such a beautiful day. It will surely cheer you up."

"You're probably right. Okay. I think I'll just take Lexie today. Daisy might struggle to keep up. I feel like a long walk."

"Sure thing." Isabel smiles. "I'll fill your water bottle."

"Thanks, Mom," replies Avery.

With everything she's gone through these past few days, Avery really feels the need to get out into nature and get some perspective on life. Reaching for Lexie's leash, she delicately pats the youngest of her pets on the head, and the two of them head out through the back door, with Avery cheerfully calling, "I promise to be back before lunch."

CHAPTER 8

IT'S A BEAUTIFUL SPRING DAY. The sun beaming through the trees makes everything sparkle, and the woodland animals all seem to be enjoying the warm weather as much as Avery is. The chirping is mesmerizing. There are at least five different types of birds competing for sound waves.

That's funny. It sounds just like when everyone tunes their instruments at the start of music class.

She sits on a large tree stump while Lexie sniffs around her feet. Avery fills Lexie's water bowl and notices a nearby chipmunk.

Poor thing. You look so stressed. Is someone chasing you? It really isn't fair that you need to die for others to survive. This reality always disturbed her. Trying to make a small difference, Avery managed to convince her family to switch to a plant-based diet about a year ago. Even though they sometimes eat meat, they try to avoid it as much as possible.

After a few minutes, Lexie notices subtle movements in the shaded undergrowth beyond the glade and heads toward the rustling leaves, with Avery following close behind. Lexie woofs softly as she discovers an inquisitive squirrel, which quickly hightails it into a nearby tree. Avery smiles, bidding the small rodent *good day*, and they continue onwards. Lexie follows a yellow butterfly, taking them away from the main path and along a small trail, leading them deeper into the woods.

As they continue to walk, a light rain starts to fall. Avery frowns, as she'd double-checked the forecast before setting off, and it was scheduled to be sunny all day. As she pulls her hoodie over her head, the sky begins to darken, and a roll of distant thunder silences the birdsong.

Avery pulls Lexie into the hollow of a rock so they can shelter from the worst of the weather, just as heavy drops begin to fall.

"Don't worry, girl. These heavy spring showers typically only last a few minutes," she reassures her companion.

As the rain sets in, the slight hollow in the rock proves to be completely inadequate, so Avery hurries back out into the rain with a reluctant Lexie in tow, in the hope of finding somewhere that will give them more protection. The rain is blinding by now, and Avery loses her footing on the slippery path, hitting her head as she falls.

CHAPTER 9

AS AVERY COMES ROUND, she tries to stand, but the ground feels like quicksand, and she is sinking deeper with every move she makes, being pulled downwards into the darkness. She struggles to free herself, but she's in too deep. A few seconds later, she lands softly on her feet in a beautiful, sunlit flower meadow with a stream of clear, blue water running through it.

She looks down at her bare feet and at the familiar blue gown, which is flowing in the light breeze. She walks a few metres and kneels to look at herself in the stream. The reflection shows her beautiful, elegant inner form once again. Avery has no idea why she has been brought to this alternate universe again, but she instinctively feels that there is nothing to fear.

She stands and sees hundreds of statuesque beings in the distance. Some are dressed in green, others in red, orange, white, purple, turquoise, and some are dressed in varying shades of blue.

Intrigued, she walks toward them. As she gets closer, she realizes that they are all holding huge flawless pearls, out of which gently pours crystal clear water, creating the stream running through the meadow.

Avery follows the stream with her eyes. The water cascades through the meadow and onwards across the countryside, flowers blooming along the banks, turning the lush, green hills into a rainbow of colours that fill the air with a light, sweet scent. The birds sing the most delightful melodies while exquisite butterflies flit between the heavenly blossoms.

This is so beautiful.

Avery instantly understands what is happening. Each being is creating life, feeding the planet with pure, loved-filled water. She feels compelled to kneel down and touch the water. As she does, a glistening, oversized pearl appears in her hands, creating a gentle waterfall that feeds into the stream. Avery feels the energy, nourishment, and happiness pouring out of her hands, while her heart fills with transcendent love.

She follows the stream with her eyes and sees the beauty that the magical power of the love-filled water has on the surrounding nature. The birds, animals, insects, trees, and flowers are abundant and living in perfect harmony. Just as she feels that her heart cannot contain any more love, a sudden burst of anxiety comes over her.

Where's Lexie? I'm not meant to be here. I need to get back home to my family.

As soon as these thoughts enter her head, she finds herself back in the forest, shivering with cold. The sky is still dark with clouds, and the rain is still pouring.

"Lexie! Lexie! Where are you? Come here, girl. Come here." Avery crawls on her hands and knees, feeling the ground around her, the sense of panic instantly melting away as a cold wet nose pushes into her face. Relieved, she grabs a hold of Lexie's leash and slowly gets to her feet. Overwhelmed, she mindlessly follows Lexie—leading her back to the main path home, to the warmth and familiarity of her grandparents' house.

CHAPTER 10

LATER THAT EVENING, Avery heads down to the basement and isn't surprised to find Teagan curled up in one of the overstuffed chairs, binge-watching her show on her tablet. Avery plonks herself down in her favourite chair and begins looking through the stack of old photo albums that are lying on the nearby table.

It doesn't take long for Avery to doze off, with images of the past dancing in her mind, pulling her into another dimension. She lets herself go. The moment she does, a mystical being appears before her. She is wearing a shimmering, turquoise, floor-length dress that is the colour of a tropical ocean found alongside dreamy island beaches. Her aquamarine eyes are accentuated by her mint-coloured hair.

The beautiful being extends a hand. Avery does the same, and instantly morphs into her true form. As she transforms, she discovers that the being is her grandmother. She throws herself into Kamila's arms and is filled with love, as both beings hug for the first time in years.

Dumbfounded, Avery opens her eyes and blinks slowly as the basement room comes into focus.

How could our hug feel so real? That wasn't just a dream. I could touch her and feel her. She looked so different, but I know it was Grandma.

"Are you okay, Ave?" Teagan interrupts her thoughts. "You look thrown. Do you miss Dad? I know I do . . ."

"No, that's not it. I know we only get to see him a few times a year. Cheer up, Teag! He promised to visit when he's back in the country at the end of the summer."

"You're right . . . okay. Then, what's up?" asks Teagan.

"I actually just had the greatest dream ever!"

"Really? What was it about?"

"Grandma gave me a hug. It felt *sooo* real." Avery grabs a tissue and dries the happy tears rolling down her cheeks.

"You're so lucky! I'd love to get a visit from Grandma! Come here," she says, walking over to hug her big sister.

"Thanks, Teag. I'll try to go back to sleep. Maybe I can dream of her again."

Avery snuggles back down and closes her eyes as more happy tears trickle down her cheeks. She feels good about having shared her dream with Teagan—part of it, at least.

I can't tell her about these wacky dreams. She'll tell Mom, and she'll send me to see a shrink. Anyway, the hug's the important part. Not where we were or what we looked like.

CHAPTER 11

AVERY DOZES OFF with the beautiful sensation of hugging her grandmother, hoping that her dreams will carry her back to the same place—and they do.

She is walking hand in hand with Kamila, their long hair and flowing dresses moving weightlessly as they stroll in a field of sweetly scented wildflowers.

"I'm so happy to be here with you. Zander told me I would see you, but I didn't know it would be this soon."

"I've been looking forward to seeing you too, sweetie. You've started to explore some of the wonders of this dimension, and I brought you here tonight so I can teach you even more."

"Brought me here? Are we still in the parallel universe?"

"Yes, we are."

"But everything looks and feels like Earth."

"We are still on Earth, but we're in a parallel dimension. Let me try to explain. You know how your phone can send messages and pictures to anyone, no matter where they are?"

Avery nods, understanding.

"They do this by using wavelengths that are invisible to the human eye. It's the same with this alternate universe. It exists, but it is invisible, because it vibrates at a frequency that is unnoticeable to humans. There could be a hundred people in this meadow in 'your' reality, but we can't see them, and they can't see us, because we're vibrating at different frequencies."

"But if we're in a different dimension, why can I still see birds flying, smell the flowers, and feel the grass beneath my feet? Why is it that humans are the only things I can't sense?"

"That's because this dimension is like an invisible shield that exists to keep Earth safe. And the only people who can distinguish it, or be perceived in it, are awoken protectors—like you and me."

"That's amazing."

"It really is."

"There's something else I don't understand, though. The field I visited earlier today, it didn't look or feel real—not like this place does."

"The reason it didn't feel the same as everything else you've experienced in this lifetime is because that place isn't on Earth. It's one of the many magical modules found in this parallel universe."

Avery looks puzzled, and Kamila winks reassuringly. "You'll come to understand in time. There's still so much my friends and I need to teach you. You'll learn about the roles each of us plays to safeguard Earth. For instance, I am a water protector. This means that my work in this dimension focuses on finding ways to ensure oceans, rivers, and lakes are pure and unpolluted. While your shade of blue means you're an animal protector."

"That's what Zander told me. My true purpose is to help safeguard animals, but I don't know what that means exactly."

"Don't worry. You'll understand, in time," Kamila says, then adds,

"For now, what you need to know is that by being your best self, you feed your inner consciousness with love, which, in turn, feeds this parallel dimension with positive energy that feeds our planet."

"Really?"

"Yes. Every small act makes a difference, whether that's holding a door open for an elderly woman, caring for a crying child, or offering to lend a hand to someone in need. And that applies to all humans, not just awoken protectors like you and me."

"It sounds so simple."

"Unfortunately, it isn't. Some people live very hard lives, and it can be difficult for them to focus on others. But if all human beings could see that every good deed has the potential to inspire others to do the same, we would live in a better place. Now that you understand this, I'd like to show you something."

Just as Kamila finishes speaking, a group of golden beings appear.

"Avery, these are the inner beings of your most cherished loved ones— our family."

They hold hands and Avery immediately recognizes each one. "Mom! Eric! Teagan! Grandpa!"

"They can't interact with you. They're not protectors."

"Is that why they're golden?"

"Yes. The fate of the world doesn't rest on their shoulders like it does on ours. I brought them here to show you that our family is interconnected. We are a true unit and always will be. We are together in this dimension, even though we are no longer together on Earth."

The golden beings fade away.

"But I don't get it. How can you bring Teagan's inner being here when she's in Grandpa's basement? How can my inner being be here when I'm sleeping in the same room as Teagan, and she has no idea I'm gone? How can you be here if you passed away? This doesn't make any sense."

"This is a hard concept to understand, but our subconscious can be in different places at once."

"What? How?"

"Your inner consciousness is here with me, but it is also on Earth, in your body, sleeping comfortably in your grandfather's basement. Correct?"

"Hmm . . . I guess so."

"Well, it's the same thing for your mother, your stepfather, and so on. That's because time is a concept invented by humans."

"What? Humans invented time?"

"Yes, they did. It's a concept that humans created to try to make sense of the world. In essence, what I'm trying to say is that time does not exist."

"Come on . . . that can't be true."

"I know this is a far-fetched concept, but you'll understand it one day."

"Okay then," she skeptically replies. "I'll try to remember that next time I'm having a bad day. Teehee!"

"Haha! Sweetheart, I know I'm throwing a lot of bizarre concepts your way, and you're doing great, but hold on to your hat. There's a lot more for you to discover."

CHAPTER 12

"HUMAN BEINGS COME to Earth to love, learn, die, and repeat."

"Repeat?"

"Yes. We all come to Earth again and again to learn a series of valuable lessons. Did you know that we have all lived many lifetimes and each of us gets to write our own story?"

"Seriously?"

"Yes. When babies are born, they come with a set of predetermined chapters—a series of events that will happen to them in their lifetime. These are the lessons their subconscious needs to learn, while their story builds on its own, day after day, week after week, year after year."

"Hold on. You said that we get to write our own story, but now you're saying that everything is preplanned. I don't get to choose? What if I break my leg or fail an exam? There's no way for me to avoid that? That's not fair. I should have a say, shouldn't I?"

Kamila nods in agreement. "Specific incidents aren't predetermined, but the lessons are. How you learn the lessons is up to you. Not too long ago, your inner being was in this dimension, trying to determine which life you should leap into, to gain the knowledge your subconscious requires."

"So, you're saying I picked my life the same way I pick a new outfit."

"I guess so, yes! After careful consideration, you chose to become *Avery*. Your inner consciousness picked your life, your book, and your chapters so you can learn a series of specific lessons. But your story isn't predetermined. You're the one who decides how to live your life."

"Okay, that makes me feel a bit better. Honestly, though, everything you're telling me sounds crazy!"

"I know, and I'm not done!" Enthusiastically, Kamila continues, "Each action you take and each decision you make has a direct impact on your life. How you react to situations either helps your subconscious grow or stay stagnant. So, when things are tough and you feel like giving up, you must remember that you're going through this for a specific reason. You must learn from what is happening to you, or around you, and act accordingly. Accepting this fate and learning to make the best of the worst kind of situation is one of the most difficult lessons to learn. But if you do, your inner consciousness will thank you, and will take care of you."

"But Grandma, what about all those people who suffer from disease, abuse, or neglect?"

"This is one of the hardest concepts to assimilate. These are horrendous hardships that no human would willingly choose to live through. Why would anyone volunteer to suffer like that? But you, as a human being, are not the one who chose this life. Your subconscious did. It isn't a big deal for your inner being to agree to a lifetime of hardship given that time does not exist."

"I guess if you look at it that way, it makes sense. But it's still hard to grasp."

"I agree. But try to remember that each event, moment, and encounter is purposely put in your path. So, we must stay strong and try to accept what is happening, even when everything seems hopeless."

"That's easier said than done."

"It truly is. Let's try something—let's pretend your boyfriend breaks up with you. How do you think you'd react?"

"Hmm . . . I'd feel sad."

"Okay. Then what?"

"Well . . . I guess I'd hang out with friends, binge-watch a bunch of movies, and go to the park. I'd keep busy and try to get over it as quickly as possible. I mean, feeling sad is no way to live, right?"

"Okay. And do you think you would succeed?"

"Yes, I'd have to."

"So, what do you think is the underlying lesson of this hypothetical scenario?"

"I guess I'd have to find a way to get over my heartbreak. I'd have to realize that my life isn't over, that I'm surrounded by people who love me, and that I'm going to be okay."

"That sounds about right. It may take one person a couple of weeks to come to that conclusion. It may take another person six months or two years. The point is, if you learn the lesson, and you face a similar situation in the future, you will be ready for it."

"Oh, I get it."

"Hold on. There's more. If you are unable to get over this heartbreak, you may instinctively bury your feelings and pretend everything's fine. So, one day, the lesson will come back. You will face a comparable scenario where someone hurts your feelings, the same way Jake did, and you'll have to try to get through it. If you're unwilling to deal with the event and disregard the lesson, it will keep coming back in one way or another."

"*Aaahhh*, now I get it."

"Wonderful. There's one last thing I'd like to tell you tonight. I showed you earlier that our family is always together in this dimension. Well, we're also always together on Earth, generation after generation."

"What do you mean?"

"Well, in one life, you and your grandfather could be cousins, and

Eric could be your uncle. In another, we could be sisters, and in another, your mother could be your lifelong best friend. But no matter the human body our subconscious chooses, our family will stay together for eternity."

"Unreal! So, does that mean that even if you're here with me right now, your inner being has already chosen a new life? Are you back on Earth? Or are you waiting for one of us to have a baby, or adopt one, or something?"

"I'm not back yet. But one day, when the time is right, I will come back to Earth. And even though I won't remember this place and all its magic, we will find each other and feel an inexplicable bond."

"Wow! That's amazing."

"I know. It's a lot to take in. I think we've covered enough for tonight." Kamila leans in and gives Avery a warm, loving hug. Then she gradually fades away as Avery continues to sleep peacefully.

CHAPTER 13

THE FOLLOWING FRIDAY, Avery waves goodbye to Eric as he drives away from the gates of the De La Grotta Zoo. She shows her access card to one of the security guards and swiftly makes her way to the locker room. "Sky, I need to talk with you."

"Hey, Ave, what's up?" Skyler looks concerned as she picks up on the urgency in Avery's voice.

Avery grabs Skyler's arm, pulls her in close, and whispers, "Something's not right."

"Not here, Ave," Skyler says nervously. "We need to feed the monkeys. Let's chat as we walk over to their enclosure."

Once the girls have prepared the buckets of fruit and vegetables, they head over to the monkey enclosure, and Avery explains what's on her mind.

"I came to the zoo yesterday after school, and three of the animals weren't in their enclosures. One of the giraffes, Herald the tiger, and the white peacock."

"Yes, I know. They took them to the new vet clinic."

"Why? What's wrong with them?"

"I don't know, but I'm sure they'll be fine, with all the high-tech equipment they have down there."

"You've been to the restricted area?"

"Oh, that's right. I haven't had a chance to tell you yet. The new owners are looking to expand the vet team, so I applied for a position as an assistant. They showed me around the restricted area when I had my interview."

"That's great!"

"I know, right! In the interview, they said if I get the position, there will be a cash bonus when I sign all the paperwork."

"Seriously?"

"Yeah! I could really use the money to help cover my university fees."

"Fingers crossed."

"And toes! I really hope it works out." Skyler smiles as they reach the monkey zone.

Shocked, Avery and Skyler look around at the enclosures.

"The chimpanzees' shelter is half-empty!" states Avery. "And where are all the capuchins?"

"I don't know . . ." anxiously replies Skyler. "All these monkeys were healthy a few months ago and now more than half of them are gone."

"What's going on?"

"I have no idea, but I heard we're getting a bunch of new monkeys in the coming weeks."

"That's good," replies Avery with a sigh of relief.

"Maybe."

"What do you mean, 'maybe'?" Avery looks at Skyler quizzically.

"They told us they were closing this area to the public for maintenance, but they haven't carried out any repairs. In the meantime, a bunch of monkeys have disappeared, and we know they don't intend on reopening the monkey zone to the public until the new shipment arrives. So, no one will ever know the original monkeys disappeared. It's as if it were planned, and as though they're trying to hide something."

"But what?"

"Beats me, but if the monkeys are getting sick, maybe they're trying to hide the fact that the vet team isn't doing a great job."

"You really think so?"

"Who knows. I mean, the vet team seems competent, but something's not adding up," Skyler sighs heavily.

"Have you spoken with the new assistant manager, Hazel? What does she think?"

"We haven't really talked about it. We've kind of been talking about other things." Skyler blushes.

"Other things?" Avery raises an eyebrow.

"Yeah, she asked me out on a date this weekend."

"Oh, wow! That's so cool! I'm really happy for you—I knew there was chemistry between the two of you." Avery gives her friend a big hug.

"Anyway," Skyler says cheerfully. Avery finally lets go of her, and Skyler continues, "We'd better get on with feeding what's left of the monkeys. We need to make sure they're staying as healthy as possible!"

The two friends quickly get to work filling the food bowls and putting fresh water into the dishes. Avery can't stop thinking about the disappearing animals. She steers the conversation back in a direction that might help her fit the puzzle pieces together.

"What did the new vet clinic look like?"

"I've never seen anything like it."

"Really?"

"Yes. It's huge, and everything looks brand new and really expensive. Hazel told me it's primarily a research laboratory, rather than a veterinary clinic."

"I wonder what they're researching."

"Who knows! But one thing's for sure—they're working with a lot of things that need to be kept cold; they've got a walk-in freezer the size of our lunchroom. But the really weird thing is the new managing director's office. There's something creepy about it."

"Mr. Fleming?"

"Yeah, that's him."

"What do you mean, 'creepy'?"

"His office doesn't have any windows."

"Well, that's not particularly unusual."

"But there are floor-to-ceiling, red velvet curtains hanging on the wall on each side of his desk."

"That *is* strange."

"But what's even creepier is that there are at least two dozen animal head trophies hanging on the walls."

"Hold on! You're saying that he's displaying dead animals in his office?"

"Yup."

"Stuffed and mounted?"

"Exactly."

"That can't be true!"

"I know. I felt sick to my stomach."

"What did Hazel say about it?"

"*Shhhh*, someone's coming . . ."

CHAPTER 14

A FEW DAYS GO BY. Avery still can't shake the eerie feeling that's been haunting her since the conversation she had with Skyler. Lying in bed, she stares at the ceiling. She sighs loudly, drags herself out of bed, and walks to her closet. Scanning through the potential outfit combinations, her mind wanders.

At least I haven't had one of those weird dreams in a while. That's one less thing to think about. It was great to see Grandma. But was that really her? It felt like it was, but she looked so different. Anyway . . . She pulls out a pair of dark jeggings and a green, sporty, three-quarter-sleeve T-shirt. *Might as well put all of those crazy dreams behind me and focus on what's real. Like trying to figure out what's happening at the zoo.*

Later that morning, Avery's struggling to focus on what her English teacher is saying. Pike nudges her gently.

Avery and Pike often pair up for class projects. He's been in love with her since third grade, but Avery has only ever had eyes for Jake. Pike can't stop himself from feeling the way he does, even though she has never given him a second thought—mostly because he still dresses like a seven-year-old boy with baggy jeans, runners, and socks that match his colourful, loose-fitting T-shirt of the day.

They've both learned to live with his endless one-way crush, because Avery truly values Pike's friendship and intellect. He's naturally brilliant with computers and electronic devices, and often spends his spare time dismantling and rebuilding gadgets.

"Listen up, everyone," announces Mr. Alvarez. "Over the coming week, you will work with a partner to come up with a two-thousand-word essay on how you see the afterlife. I won't prescribe how you should write your paper. What I care about is that you build a strong case that clearly explains your thoughts. I will also be looking for properly structured sentences and paragraphs."

"Hey, Ave. I have a bunch of ideas. You want to pair up?"

Perplexed, Avery gawks at Pike. "Umm . . . what?"

"Are you okay?"

"Umm . . . yeah, sorry. Sure, let's meet up at lunch."

"Now that everyone seems to have found a partner," says Mr. Alvarez, "let's open our books to page 253."

Avery can't focus. Wide-eyed, she bites her nails and stares in wonder, completely overwhelmed by deep thoughts.

What are the odds? Just when I decide to put all of this behind me, it pops back up. And . . . I mean . . . I have all the answers . . . the real answers. Why did Mr. Alvarez choose this topic for our essay?

She furrows her brow before looking at her partner and exhaling deeply.

Thank goodness I'll be working with Pike on this one. He crushes so hard on me that no matter how ridiculous my ideas may seem, I'm pretty sure he'll at least indulge in the conversation.

CHAPTER 15

AT LUNCH, AVERY SITS cross-legged on the grass with Pike beside her, his arms wrapped around his knees. Avery is struck by how close Pike's ideas about the afterlife are to her experiences, even though she figures he's basing his thinking on the numerous comic books he loves to read. She listens in silence as he talks enthusiastically about how he believes we live side by side in multiple alternate dimensions, where everyday decisions create different paths for our inner consciousness to tread.

"In my mind," he says thoughtfully, "we're all living on Earth for a short period of time, and we do this to achieve a common goal. I don't know what the goal is exactly, but I know we're not here for nothing. Can you imagine if the theory of parallel dimensions is true and there are hundreds of versions of 'you' out there? Think about it! You live happily in your family. Then, one day, you get a baby brother. You develop a deep bond with him, and you would do anything to keep him safe. This is one life option. In another, you don't get along with your brother, and you become enemies. This is a different life path. So now, in the universe, there are two scenarios running side by side for your subconscious to learn from. And every time either of these 'Averys' makes a life-changing decision, a new scenario is born. This goes on, again and again, until you die."

"Gee, Pike. That's a hard concept to grasp!" Avery widens her eyes innocently, as though these ideas are new to her.

"I know it sounds crazy, but let your imagination go to a new level with it, and it makes sense," Pike says earnestly.

"I think it's really cool. It's just a bit hard to get. So, you're saying that there could be a nice Avery and a mean one?"

"Yes, and even several hundred versions of each."

"I have a hard time believing that. I can't even hurt a fly. I stepped on a spider once and cried for fifteen minutes. I don't see how I could ever be purposefully mean, even if it were in a separate life path. It's just not in my nature. I can't even understand what makes people act badly. I just don't get it."

"It's probably because you're so pure-hearted, and you haven't been exposed to a lot of awful things in your life."

"Hmm. Maybe. I'm not that innocent, though. I think I've met some pretty bad people."

"What are you talking about?"

"I think there's something creepy going on at the De La Grotta Zoo. I don't trust the new owners. Something feels off."

"Okay, sorry. I take it back. That does sound troubling. But the fact that you gave this as an example proves my point. It's hard for people like you and me to imagine how others may live or feel. There's a lot of suffering out there. Some folks don't have enough to eat or don't have anywhere to live. Others are so stressed by everything they must do to ensure their family survives that they never get a break—they never have a chance to relax and enjoy life. Can you imagine living like that?"

"No, I can't. That must be awful."

"Exactly. Check this out. A few months ago, I overheard my parents talking in the living room, and my mom was crying. You know that she's a detective, right?" asks Pike.

"Yeah. I mean, I thought she was a regular cop, not a detective."

"Okay, well, this happened when she was still on general patrol, before she became a detective. Some days were so hard on her that she would come home and have long talks with my dad, because she couldn't handle it anymore. They would whisper, but I could still hear what they were saying. That day, she was crying because she'd had to arrest a man for stealing groceries. She felt bad for him, but she didn't have a choice. She had to do her job, even though he explained that he didn't know what else to do. There wasn't any food left to feed his children. He told my mom that he and his wife worked over forty hours a week at the same company, but they still couldn't make ends meet. He also said how unfair it was that they got paid minimum wage, while the company's bosses each made over half a million dollars a year."

"That's not cool!"

"No, it isn't," Pike continues passionately. "It's really unfair. This hard-working dad ended up in jail because he needed to provide for his family. The point that I'm trying to make is that even though I believe we should all try to do the best we can, we need to remember that it's easier for some people than it is for others."

"That's so true," Avery nods thoughtfully. "If the rich, greedy, egocentric people stopped focusing on themselves, they could decide to use their power and influence to change the world for the better. Just like that time my mom was hired by a lady who had just bought a clothing line and wanted to find a way to pay her new employees more fairly. They cut the salaries of the senior executives and used that money to double the hourly rate of all minimum-wage staff. Some of the big bosses weren't happy, and threatened to leave the company, but the new owner stood her ground and implemented my mom's plan."

"That's amazing. Can you imagine if the guy my mom arrested for shoplifting worked at that company instead of the other one? He wouldn't have had to steal food to feed his family, and he would still be at home rather than in jail."

"Yeah, seriously."

"I wish more people believed in karma and reincarnation. Maybe they'd act differently and think twice before hurting others."

Avery sees an opportunity to let Pike into her confidence. "Exactly! Hey, I have this theory, where we each choose our life to learn a series of lessons."

"Oh, wow! That sounds interesting. Tell me about it!" Pike looks at Avery attentively.

"Okay, so, in my mind, somewhere in the universe, we are each waiting for the right time to be born. We choose where and when to go, picking the best family to help us master what we need to learn in the next lifetime. It's like looking at a series of books in a library. You look at the picture, you glance at the title, and you may even read the back cover so you have a general idea of what the book is about, but you don't know how the story will unfold until you start making your way through it."

"That's so cool. Where did this idea come from?"

"I've been carrying it in me since I was a kid," Avery replies, half truthfully. *And a paranormal being—who might, or might not, be my grandma—confirmed it a few days ago.*

"I'm so lucky to have you as a friend. I've never talked to anyone else about these things." Pike smiles. "I love that you're so open-minded."

"Well, it is the topic of our essay, after all."

"Yeah, but still. If I would've been paired up with someone else, I never would have shared all I did. Most people would laugh at our ideas."

"That's true!"

"But with you, it's different. We both believe in wacky things, and we're okay with that."

"I never thought of it that way. I'm the one who decides my truth. If I discover something far-fetched in a dream, and it feels real to me, it can be." Avery looks at Pike gratefully.

"That's right, and for me, that's when you know you genuinely believe in something. It's that feeling deep down in your gut when you know you're right even though you can't prove it. When you own that conviction, no one can ever take it away from you."

"Gee, Pike. I think we'll ace this paper." Avery grabs her phone and looks at the time. "The bell's about to go. We'd better run. Let's meet up after school to keep working on our project."

"Sure thing!" Pike smiles from ear to ear, happy to spend so much time with Avery.

CHAPTER 16

THE NEXT WEEK, Pike and Avery nervously hand in their homework. It is so wild that they figure they will either ace it or flunk it. After school, Avery drops by the local park, wanting to surround herself with nature, as she's feeling anxious about the assignment.

What if Mr. Alvarez reads our paper in class and everybody thinks our ideas are stupid? What if he starts asking me all types of questions I don't want to answer?

Avery suddenly feels exposed, and regrets being so honest with Pike and, moreover, for writing it all in an essay. She sits down under a big oak tree, closes her eyes, and tries to clear her mind. Countless images, words, and thoughts flash through her brain. Distracted, she opens her eyes and looks up. The tree is filled with small leaves that will reach their full potential when the warmer weather finally arrives.

Closing her eyes again, she breathes in the crisp spring air.

Come on, Avery. You can do this. She tries to remember Ms. Gupta's meditation instructions. *Avery, imagine yourself on a deserted beach. Feel the sand under your feet. Feel the heat of the sun.*

She takes an even deeper breath and focuses on the feeling of the breeze on her face. *It's working! It feels as though I'm walking barefoot in warm, cozy, sand . . . I think.* Trying to stay in the zone, she focuses on the sound of gentle waves crashing on shore. She begins to relax and feels her entire body quiver. Noticing a beautiful tint of turquoise in her mind's eye, she moves toward it. When she gets close enough to touch it, her grandmother's inner consciousness appears.

"Grandma. Is that really you? I haven't had a dream in almost a week. I didn't know if I'd get to see you again."

"It's me. Come here, sweetie."

Avery jumps into her grandmother's arms and instantly morphs into her metaphysical state, while their surroundings transform into a beautiful sunlit forest. She hears a soft symphony of bird calls, lifts her head, closes her eyes, and extends her arms as she inhales deeply and smells fresh mint and strawberry aromas that tickle her nose.

"Avery, my sweet. You truly are one of the most loving individuals I've ever known. You're so beautiful, both inside and out."

"I miss you so much. I think of you every single day. You left us too quickly. I know I must move on with my life, but it's hard." Tears trickle down Avery's cheeks.

"Oh, sweetie. I'm here with you."

"Yes, but you'll leave again. It's not fair."

"Look around you." Kamila smiles gently. "What do you see?"

"I see trees, grass, and clear blue skies."

"Do you see where we are?"

"We're in the alternate universe again."

"That's right. But in your reality, you are sitting under a big oak tree in your favourite park. Correct?"

"Yes, I am. I'm sitting in a park, but I'm also standing here with you."

"Exactly. As I explained last time, your inner consciousness can be in multiple places at once. Anytime you wish to see me, simply take a few minutes, relax, and call for me. I'm always here for you, and I always will be."

Avery still can't stop the tears from falling, but she nods to show she understands.

"I'd like to show you something. I have a feeling it will cheer you up," Kamila says softly.

"Okay," Avery replies, trying to control her emotions.

Kamila takes Avery's hand, and they immediately find themselves hovering a few metres above crystal clear water.

"This is gorgeous. I can see all the way to the bottom. Look at all the brightly coloured fish! I've never seen anything like it."

"You want to go for a swim?" asks Kamila, her face lighting up with excitement.

"Can I, really?"

"Of course! What are you waiting for? Dive in! You'll be fine. I promise."

Avery takes a deep breath and dives headfirst into the tropical waters. She quickly realizes that she can breathe underwater. Diving deeper, Avery catches a glimpse of Kamila swimming gracefully with a shoal of colourful angel fish. Avery's eyes widen as she realizes that her grandmother has morphed into a mermaid.

CHAPTER 17

SERIOUSLY?

Kamila smiles and gently grabs Avery's hand. They both vanish and land softly on a small, deserted island not too far away.

"As a water protector, I can become a mermaid whenever I want and swim wherever my heart takes me."

"That's so cool!"

"It really is. It's the best part of being a water protector. And as a water guardian, I can also bestow the ability to breathe underwater on protectors who are swimming with me."

"That's amazing! But what do you mean by 'water guardian'?"

"Oh! Have I forgotten to teach you about that?" asks Kamila.

"I guess so." Avery shrugs.

"Have you noticed that Zander and I look a bit different than you do?"

"Now that you mention it, your hair and eye colour match your outfits and mine don't."

"That's right. This is how you can easily distinguish a guardian from a protector. There is only one guardian for each of Earth's seven foundational components—Earth, air, water, plants, humans, animals, and insects. I'm the water guardian, and Zander is the plant guardian.

As guardians, we are the only beings able to evoke humans to their innate calling, and we must do so while also watching over protectors."

"That must keep you busy," Avery snickers.

"It sure does, but time doesn't exist. Remember?" winks Kamila.

"Oh, yeah!" Avery smiles. "Anyhow, I wish I could become a mermaid."

"That would be wonderful! Although you can't be a mermaid, as an animal protector, you, too, are a shapeshifter."

"Really?"

"Yes. You possess the innate ability to morph into an animal. It is the only way you can truly safeguard what you are meant to protect."

"That's incredible. How do I shift?"

"Close your eyes. Imagine yourself in the most peaceful place possible. Don't try to direct your thoughts. Let your heart guide you," Kamila instructs. "Now, tell me what you see."

"I see endless blue skies. I see white, fluffy clouds all around me. Grandma! I'm flying!"

"What else do you see? Look at your hands, your body, your feet."

"I'm covered in feathers! This is incredible!!"

"Look around you. Is there somewhere you can land and see your reflection?"

Avery examines the ground below. "Everything's so clear. It's like looking through Grandpa's binoculars. I just saw a rabbit jump out of a small bush. And over there, two squirrels are chasing each other. This is completely nuts!" She raises her gaze and adds, "Oh, I see water. I'll fly there now."

She makes her way over the thick forest with grace and agility, landing on a fallen tree that overhangs a small pond. She leans over and gapes into the still water. Dark, intense black and yellow eyes stare back at her. Her head is covered with dark-brown, silky feathers, and her beak looks as though it could easily pierce through metal.

"Grandma, I'm a falcon!"

"Beautiful!" Kamila says joyfully. "Whenever you're in this dimension and you feel like taking flight, simply close your eyes and allow your heart to guide you."

"I can go anywhere in the world?"

"That's right. Close your eyes and let yourself go," Kamila says encouragingly.

Avery's inner being vanishes from the deserted island and reappears as a falcon on a secluded rooftop. She instinctively lifts her wings to cover her face as though this will shield her from any potential harm—the same way she hid under her blankie as a toddler whenever thunder would roar.

What am I doing? I'm sure there's nothing to worry about. Avery slowly lowers her wings and sees darkness. *Why is it nighttime? Oh . . . it's the time difference. That means it worked!*

Avery flaps her wings and immediately takes flight. Within a few seconds, she is high enough to see that she is flying above the Cathédrale Notre-Dame de Paris.

I'm here. I'm truly here. I'm in Paris. This is fabulous!

She swoops toward the Louvre Museum.

I wish Mom could be here with me right now. She's always talked about visiting the Louvre to see the Mona Lisa in real life.

Staying high, so she doesn't attract attention, Avery flies above the Seine River, making her way to the Arc de Triomphe, and finally to the Eiffel Tower, where she finds a secluded spot to perch.

This is sooo cool! I can't believe it!

Avery closes her eyes again and lets her heart guide her. She feels feels warm, dry air, and even before she opens her eyes again, she realizes she is no longer in Europe. She opens her eyes to find that it's nighttime, although there is a faint yellow tint from the ground below.

I'm in the desert!

Avery soars to a great height, looks around, and quickly sees three remarkable pyramids.

This is sooo wild! I need to get a closer look. This is completely mesmerizing. I know where to go next.

She finds a secluded spot where she can disappear without anyone noticing, closes her eyes, and reappears in a lush evergreen tree, high up on a mountain. It is daytime. She knows right away that she is exactly where she wanted to go. She takes flight, trying to decide which of the letters in the iconic *Hollywood* sign to perch herself on. She lands on the middle point of the *W* and looks at the city where all her favourite movies were made.

This is insane! Teag would be sooo jealous if she knew I were here. I wish I could tell her all about this. She would lose it, for sure.

Avery decides to stay in California, and flies toward the nearby Pacific Ocean, where a group of five falcons are swooping and soaring in the warm air currents. She gets closer, joining the flock, overwhelmed by the view, the smells, the sounds, and the weightlessness.

After a while, she leaves the group and perches under the Malibu Pier, inhaling the warm, salty ocean air. She closes her eyes and finds herself back on the deserted island, sitting alongside her grandmother's shimmering, turquoise mermaid being.

CHAPTER 18

"OH, GRANDMA, that was amazing! I really felt like I was there."

"That's because you were. And you've only just started to scratch the surface of the endless possibilities that lie within this dimension."

Avery closes her eyes as Kamila kisses her beloved granddaughter on the forehead. When she opens them again, the blue sky is peeping through the branches of the oak tree. She quickly shuts her eyes, hoping to return to her meditative state—and it works. She is back in the alternate dimension.

There's one more place I want to see before I head back home.

Avery follows her heart, and morphs into her inner falcon, perched in the branches of the oak tree.

She takes flight and aims for the De La Grotta Zoo, soaring in the bright blue sky above a sea of clouds that look like misshaped cotton balls. She tucks her wings and dives headfirst into the tiniest cloud she can find. While it dissipates, she looks for another target and aims headfirst. Poof. The cloud scatters. Feeling adventurous, she expands her wings and flies just above the tree tops, close enough that she could touch them if she wanted to, and lands on the zoo's highest rooftop.

She looks down, admiring the animals. *They look so small—even the giraffes and the elephants. This is unreal!* She sees Skyler walking across the courtyard toward the reptile house, carrying a bucket, and dressed in one of the lab coats that are only worn by the new veterinary staff.

It looks like Sky got the assistant vet job. Good for her! She must be super happy.

Avery instinctively calls to her friend, "Hey, Sky, did you get the job?"

Intrigued by the *kak, kak, kak* call coming from above, Skyler looks up. "Hey there, beautiful. What are you doing here? Ah, I know. I bet you want one of these rats. Sorry. These aren't for you. They're for the pythons."

Yuk, no! I'll pass, thank you!

Skyler pushes open the door to the reptile house and disappears inside. Avery scans the rest of the zoo and notices two well-groomed middle-aged men dressed in expensive looking suits speaking near one of the empty enclosures. She flies down and lands on the top of the nearest shelter.

"When are we getting more monkeys?" asks Mr. Fleming. "We need at least twice as many to meet this month's demand."

"The shipment has been delayed at the border. They'll be arriving next week."

"Excellent. Add a few to these enclosures so we can reopen the monkey zone without raising any questions."

"Of course."

"Are we ready for tomorrow's event?"

"Yes, sir. We're booked to capacity—the full one hundred and fifty people. The chefs are putting the finishing touches to the dishes—tiger tartar, gorilla confit, slow-roasted penguin flippers, and panda escalope. For those who enjoy sweet indulgences, we will also be serving sea turtle egg meringue, with a lime coulis."

Avery screams in horror at what she's hearing. The two men lift their heads to look at the squawking falcon.

"Is that one of ours?" asks Mr. Fleming.

"No, sir. We don't have any falcons."

"If someone manages to catch it, bring it straight to the restricted area."

"Certainly, sir. If I may, I have a few more points I'd like to brief you on."

"Yes, of course, Mr. Perdue. Please, go on."

"The preparations for the summer VIP event are progressing well. The invitations were sent out two weeks ago, and we have already reached our maximum capacity of fifteen participants. They are scheduled to tour the zoo in the coming weeks to choose their kill."

"Please let me know when they arrive. I want to greet them in person."

"Yes, sir. I will ask your assistant to add the appointments to your schedule. You will also be pleased to know that Hazel has recruited one of the original staff members. Hopefully, this will hinder the rumour mill so the keepers we haven't replaced yet will stop asking awkward questions. Her name is Skyler. Once I handed her the five-thousand-dollar signing bonus, she was more than happy to sign the confidentiality agreement."

Sky's one of them? What's going on?

"The schedule for dismissing the rest of the original staff has been finalized now. It's staggered over the coming six months. We simply can't fire any more employees at this stage. It would raise too many suspicions."

Bewildered, Avery pulls herself out of her meditation and reaches for her phone, sending Skyler a text message to see if she can get any insight into whether her friend is being manipulated or if she actually knows what's going on and doesn't care about the animals.

She texts, "*Hey Sky, I heard from one of the volunteers that you were wearing a lab coat today. Did you get the assistant vet position?*"

Waiting impatiently for Skyler's reply, Avery slowly makes her way home, grabbing her phone from her bag as soon as she hears the message alert.

"*Yes! I got it!! I'm so happy, Ave! They gave me the most amazing bonus! And I still get to mentor you on Friday afternoons. So, it's all good :)*"

Avery sighs. It's impossible to tell from Skyler's reply whether or not she knows what's going on at the zoo. She'll have to wait until she sees Skyler face-to-face. She sighs again at the thought of missing this week's volunteer shift.

Why can't we leave for Grandpa's tomorrow morning instead of right after school?

She loves being at her grandfather's, but she hates the idea of having to wait a whole week to see Skyler and find out what's going on.

CHAPTER 19

ON SATURDAY MORNING, Avery slips out of bed, taking care not to wake Teagan. She grabs one of Kamila's fluffy nightgowns from the back of the bedroom door and quietly tiptoes through the house. Her grandfather is already up, sitting in a comfy chair by the living room's large bay window.

"Join me, sweetie. The sunrise is breathtaking. Look over there—hues of pinks and yellows are peeking through the dark-blue sky."

Avery leans over and gives her grandfather a hug before snuggling up in the other comfy chair.

"I'm surprised to see you up this early, darling." Marcus peers at her, over his glasses, and takes a sip of his tea.

"I was hoping we could talk for a bit before everyone wakes up."

"Of course, sweetheart," he replies. "What's on your mind?"

"There's something strange happening at the zoo where I volunteer, and it's freaking me out."

"Okay. I'm all ears, sweetie," he states. "We'll try to figure this out together."

She tells him about the strange events she's observed these past few weeks, and he listens attentively.

"Animals held in captivity fall ill, even under the best care. I'm sure things aren't as bad as they seem."

"There's more to it than that. I just know it, Grandpa! I overheard some folks talking about killing some of the animals."

"I sure hope you misunderstood. But just in case, you should keep poking around. Maybe you'll discover something that can actually be reported on."

"Okay . . ."

"Sweetie, is there something else that's bothering you?"

She takes a deep breath as she looks down at her hands, instinctively bringing one to her mouth. She immediately starts biting her nails. She tries to stop herself. She knows this is a bad habit, but she can't help it when she gets anxious.

"What I'm about to tell you will sound completely bonkers."

"You know me. I'm always up for a good story," he replies, winking and smiling.

This is true. Marcus's head is filled with mind-blowing ideas based on the countless books he's read over his lifetime, most of which were written by philosophers and eccentric thinkers.

She takes another deep breath.

"Recently, I've been dreaming that I visit a parallel universe in which I transform into an animal protector. I've been told that I have to find a way to protect animals and help save Earth. I can also shapeshift into a falcon and fly anywhere in the world."

Avery's grandfather listens attentively as his beloved granddaughter tells her tale. She's having a hard time figuring out what he's thinking. Staring at her nails, regretting every nibble, and waiting for a reaction, warm tears trickle down her cheeks.

"This is incredible." Her grandfather smiles. "These visions didn't come from your imagination. They were sent to you."

"You really think so?" she replies nervously. "Everything seems real when I'm there, but then, when I'm here, it just feels like a dream. I feel like I'm losing my mind."

"Oh, my sweet girl. I appreciate that this is a lot for you to take in, but there's no need for you to be afraid. You wouldn't have been able to discover this dimension if you weren't ready to do so."

"Really?"

"Yes. That's how it works." They both lean back in their comfy chairs.

Avery sighs deeply with her eyes closed and repeatedly shakes her head. "If what you're saying is true, then I need to find a way to help the animals. But I'm just a kid. How am I supposed to do that?"

"You could start by trying to figure out what's happening at the zoo. Maybe you could speak with someone you trust."

"The only person I thought I could talk to just became one of them."

"Follow your instincts, sweetheart." Her grandfather smiles. "Maybe you'll find an unexpected ally."

Avery hears Teagan thumping down the stairs, followed by the thunder of their two dogs.

Avery's grandfather leans forward in his chair and whispers, "Let's get up early again tomorrow morning and go for a walk so we can keep talking about this. Okay?"

Avery nods gratefully just as Teagan and the dogs come charging into the living room.

CHAPTER 20

EARLY THE NEXT MORNING, Marcus softly knocks on the girls'
bedroom door, peaks his head in, and whispers, "Avery, sweetie. Are you
up?"

"I'm awake," Avery mumbles sleepily, still tucked in bed. "I'll be ready
in five minutes."

Hurriedly pulling on a pair of jeans and a hoodie and tying her hair
back into a messy ponytail, Avery stumbles into the living room, where
her grandfather is sitting in his chair by the window. After a quick cup
of tea, the pair head out into the quiet early morning, the chill of the
night still hanging in the air as the sun creeps over the rooftops of the
neighbouring houses.

"I dreamt of Grandma again last night. She reached out to me so we
could hold hands. When we did, a floating crystal ball appeared between
us. The instant I grabbed it, it lit up and started to show moments from
my childhood."

"That's amazing, sweetie."

Avery glances over at her grandfather. His face is pale, and he looks as though he's in pain.

"Are you feeling okay? Do you need to head back home?"

"No. I think I just need to sit down," he reassures her. He settles onto a tree stump, and Avery sits on the ground beside him, resuming her story.

"After a few minutes, the images stopped changing. They froze on a memory of me when I was six years old. I was standing in your kitchen with Grandma, and we were both wearing aprons. It's the memory of the first time I ever baked a cake. Do you remember that day, Grandpa?"

"Yes! I do! It was to celebrate my sixty-fifth birthday," he replies with a warm smile.

"In my dream, Grandma reminded me that I wanted to make a purple and green cake with bubble-gum ice cream layers, and that she'd finally convinced me to bake a simple chocolate sponge with whipped cream and fresh strawberries."

"That's right! She didn't want to hinder your imagination, but she wanted to ensure you'd bake a cake I would actually eat. What a lovely memory."

"There's more." Avery gently takes her grandfather's hands, and they are instantly transported to an alternate dimension.

Dumbfounded, he turns to his granddaughter and asks in wonder, "Is this truly happening?"

"I guess so. If there's one thing I've learned these past few weeks, it's that it's better to try to relax and just enjoy being here," she says softly, remembering how strange it felt when she first found herself in this parallel world.

Avery feels his hands loosen their grip on hers—relaxing. He looks down and sees that he is holding a magical sphere. He also sees that he is no longer human. He has transformed into his innate shape—a tall, golden creature.

"Oh my. This is incredible."

The globe shows an image of Avery as a three-month-old baby snuggling in his arms. A few seconds later, the picture changes. This time, it shows Avery as a five-year-old girl in the park near his house. The image changes again. This time, an unfamiliar scene appears. Avery looks closer.

"That's strange. I don't think this is a memory, but I feel as though I've seen this image before, but I can't recognize any of the people."

She looks up from the crystal ball and sees that her grandmother has joined them. Her grandfather's eyes are filled with love and tears.

"Kamila, my beloved. Is it really you?"

Kamila looks deep into her husband's eyes. Without saying a word, she takes the magical sphere and places it in Avery's hands. She gives her husband the most loving hug, and they reconnect as though they never parted.

A few moments later, Kamila looks at Avery and says, "Don't you recognize this memory?"

"How can I? I thought these were all my memories. But this seems to be the memory of a man I don't know."

"Keep looking. You'll figure it out."

Avery carefully examines the young man, who is dressed in a police uniform.

"Is that . . . me?" she asks, her voice tinged with confusion.

"Yes, darling. This is you in the life you led two lifetimes ago. You were a police officer, in charge of the K-9 unit. You saved many lives and received a medal of honour for improving the way K-9 officers treat and train their dogs."

"Whoa! That's so cool."

"The crystal ball shows memories from all your lives, not just this one."

"That's awesome. Can we see more?"

At that moment, the image changes to a rancher sitting on a striking black stallion in a field of sheep. The rancher is a lovely middle-aged woman with a long silver braid that sticks out from under her dark-brown cowboy hat.

The image morphs and depicts a veterinary school in the early nineteen hundreds with one young woman sitting in a classroom filled with men.

"That's me. I remember being ostracized. Being a female veterinarian back then was not a popular career choice, but I couldn't care less."

The image alters again. This time, Avery is a man. He is standing at the bow of a large vessel in the middle of the ocean. He is dressed in what seems to be a marine uniform with a badge on his left shoulder that reads *Head of the Marine Wildlife Protection Program.*

"It's fascinating," Marcus interjects. "All your careers focus on helping animals."

"You're right!" she replies enthusiastically, and the image dissolves again, quickly replaced by one of a baby lying on a blanket in a meadow.

A beautiful woman smiles tenderly at the baby. Avery can't tell what year this is, or which lifetime, but it doesn't matter. The love and happiness she feels is overwhelmingly positive.

"This must have been my mother, and those must be my three brothers running and playing with the beach ball." Avery guesses.

Completely amazed, Marcus declares, "Oh my! That woman is my mother!"

"You mean Grandpa was my brother?" Avery asks Kamila.

"Yes. You two were siblings," she replies.

"It's hard to believe," jumps in Marcus, "but I remember that day as though it was yesterday. Mom loved you so much. You were her perfect little angel. Your name was Margot. You only lived six months. Mom tried to move on, but she was never the same."

Avery opens her eyes and finds herself sitting beside the tree stump. She gently rubs her grandfather's forearm. He opens his eyes, shaking his head in disbelief.

"In all my life, I never thought I would experience anything like this. You helped me reconnect with your grandmother. I can't thank you enough."

"I don't think I can take the credit for this," Avery replies with a smile. "I'm pretty sure Grandma planned the whole thing."

Marcus smiles back. "Well, one thing's for sure. You can't waste this gift. Now that you know your life's purpose, you have to find a way to achieve it."

"You're right. I have to stop thinking that these are just wild dreams. This is really happening to me."

CHAPTER 21

THE FOLLOWING FRIDAY AFTERNOON, Avery lies on her bedroom floor next to Shadow, who is purring loudly while she mindlessly strokes his chin. She thinks about the last few days.

It was so amazing to share my secret with Grandpa. It's like a huge weight has been lifted from my shoulders. And then, back at school, Pike and I found out we got an A+ on our essay. Plus, things are going really well with Jake.

As she stares at the ceiling, her thoughts turn to Skyler. Her expression becomes clouded as she fills with anxiety.

Shoot! I hate this! I usually look forward to my volunteer shift and seeing Skyler, but I still don't know what's happening with her—or with the zoo. I need to figure out what's going on. Oh, I know!

She glances at her phone. *Three-thirty. I have an hour before my shift starts. Perfect. I've got time.* She closes her eyes and tries to follow her heart, but no luck.

That's weird. Why isn't this working?

She takes a deep breath and tries again. Her doorknob quickly turns, and Teagan abruptly walks in.

"Hey, sis. What's up? Why are you lying on the floor?"

"Haven't you ever heard of knocking!"

"Yeah, whatever." Teagan sits next to her big sister and starts petting Shadow, who's made his way between the two sisters in an attempt to garner even more affection. "Seriously. What are you doing?"

"I'm trying to meditate. Go away!"

"No. I want to try it."

"It won't work if you stick around. Teag, come on. You're driving me nuts! Please leave."

"Let me stay. I promise I'll be quiet."

"Aarrgg! Okay, but you can't make a sound."

"What app are you using?"

"What do you mean, 'what app'?"

"Abby's mom uses a guided meditation app. It lasts about ten minutes, and then, she's done."

"Okay, then. Can you download the app for me?" Avery hands her phone over to her little sister, who locates and downloads the app and quickly hands it back.

Avery taps on the meditation of the day icon and looks over at her sister who is sitting in a yoga pose, with her eyes closed and a huge grin on her face, with Shadow comfortably nested in her legs. Avery rolls her eyes and shakes her head.

I should be nicer. Look at her. She's so happy to hang out with me—

Avery's thoughts are interrupted by the calming voice. Both Avery and Teagan slowly sway back and forth as if they are being gently pulled and pushed by the ocean waves heard in the background.

Within a few seconds, she feels herself pull into the alternate dimension. She morphs into her inner falcon and materializes perched on a large tree near the De La Grotta Zoo's *welcome* sign.

It worked. I did it!

She expands her wings, takes flight, and soars high enough to see the entire zoo. A stream of trucks enter and exit the restricted area.

I wonder what they're moving. That big one looks like a water tanker.

She follows the driver as he leaves the zoo, driving straight to the riverbank, where he extends a massive pipe deep into the river. From high above, she notices the surrounding water immediately change colour. *Yuk! What's that smell?* The driver leans against the tanker and starts fiddling with his phone.

"Hey, you!" Avery shouts, "What are you doing?!"

He lifts his head, looks at the loud squawking falcon, and goes back to his phone.

Oh, no! The zoo must be responsible for the chemical spill that was on the news a few weeks ago! What's going on?

Avery decides she's seen enough. She opens her eyes and jumps to her feet, startling Teagan.

"What are you doing? The guy's still talking."

"Umm . . . I just remembered that I have to walk to the zoo today, so I have to get going."

There's just enough time for her to walk the long way to the zoo— along the riverbank. Maybe seeing things up close will provide some answers.

CHAPTER 22

AS SHE'S WALKING to the river, Avery's message alert pings. It's Skyler.

It reads, "*Can you come in early? We need to talk. Now!*"

Avery replies with a thumbs up, and reluctantly changes direction. *What does she want? I still can't believe she's one of them. I was sure she wanted to help animals, not hurt them. I guess I need to accept that it's almost impossible to truly know anyone . . .*

The minute she walks into the locker room, Skyler throws her arms around Avery's neck. "Ave, I'm so happy to see you."

"Hey, Sky," Avery replies cautiously. Skyler has never greeted her so enthusiastically. She takes a step back and looks at the older girl. She has tears in her eyes. "What's going on, Sky? What's wrong?" Avery is concerned now. She can see that Skyler is distressed.

"It's Kiki and Koko," she whispers, her voice choking with tears.

"What about them?" Avery asks, but she thinks she already knows the answer.

"Mr. Perdue, the general manager, said they passed away this afternoon."

Avery's eyes fill with tears the moment the words leave Skyler's lips.

"What happened?"

"He said they'd had seizures."

"What? Both of them? At exactly the same time? I don't believe it." Avery wipes away her tears and then turns to look at Skyler, whose expression is one of pure devastation.

"Are you okay?" Avery looks carefully at her friend, anxiously awaiting her reply.

"No. I hate my new job."

Avery breathes a sigh of relief.

"I can't tell you what they're doing to the animals, Ave, because I signed a confidentiality agreement. I don't know what to do. I feel completely trapped."

"I know what they're doing to the animals." Avery feels sick.

"How could you know?" Skyler replies.

"It doesn't matter how, but trust me—I know. The animals are ending up on people's plates."

"You *do* know!" Skyler's eyes widen in amazement.

Everything she overheard was true. They really have been using the animals to create menus to entertain the sick-minded elite.

"Oh, Avery, it's so awful. I'm freaking out."

"Are you really? Or is this all part of their plan?"

"What do you mean?"

"You're one of them now. Aren't you?"

"NO! I'm NOT! I promise."

"Then what about your new girlfriend, Hazel? I don't want to be mean, but I heard that the only reason she approached you for the new job is to help convince us that the zoo is in capable hands."

"Gee . . . I knew there was something off with her. She's always asking me a bunch of personal questions, and when I try to do the same, she manages to change the topic."

"If that's true, then why haven't you broken up with her?"

"I haven't had the guts to do it yet. I'm afraid of what might happen if I don't pretend like I'm okay with everything."

"Are you being honest with me? How can I be sure?"

"I'm not playing you. I promise." Skyler tears up. "I truly don't know what to do."

"Okay, okay, I believe you." Avery gives Skyler a hug. "I'm so relieved. I was worried you were one of them. I didn't know if I could trust you anymore."

"Thanks for believing me," Skyler says quietly.

"There's another VIP event coming up soon, but only fifteen people are invited this time. Have you heard anything about it?"

"Yes. Mr. Perdue has already started making a list of potential animals. And yesterday, when I went to the restricted area to pick up some equipment, I snuck a peek inside a room that looks just like a hunting arena."

"I don't get it. What do you mean?" asks Avery.

"The room is filled with fake trees, grass, boulders, and two ponds. It looks as though it's set up for people to pretend they're hunting in the wild."

"You've got to be kidding me! That can't be true."

"But what's worse is Kiki and Koko. They're not dead!"

"WHAT?" Avery looks confused. "You just told me that Mr. Perdue told everyone they both had seizures and died."

"I saw them with my own eyes a few minutes before you got here. It's why I messaged you. They're not dead. Mr. Perdue was lying. They've been moved to the restricted area, and so were a bunch of penguins. They don't even have water to swim in, and the room's way too hot for them. They're suffering, for sure."

Avery begins to cry again. "These people are horrible."

"I know." Skyler looks at the floor. "What are we going to do?"

Avery shakes her head slowly. "I don't know, but we've got to do something."

CHAPTER 23

THAT NIGHT, AVERY LIES in her bed, worrying about the animals at the zoo. As she drifts into sleep, her subconscious enters the alternate dimension. This time, she ends up standing on the moon, surrounded by a palatial, black sky filled with blue, green, and red nebulae, accentuated by dabs of white lights that dance in the distance. Three statuesque figures walk toward her.

The first is quite handsome with his dark purple, clean-cut, faded beard that matches his long hair tied in a messy bun. He is wearing a T-shirt and a sporty-chic topcoat over a pair of ripped, slim-fit jeans and matching low-cut boots. The second could be featured on the cover of a wedding magazine with her exquisite, pure-white gown, platinum eyes, and pewter-coloured hair. And the third looks like a massive fiery-orange bodybuilder who features striking amber eyes and a strawberry-blond, messy, crew cut. He is dressed in an untucked, buttoned shirt with rolled-up sleeves set over a pair of skinny jeans and fashionable runners.

"Hi, Avery. My name is Tate," says the dark-purple being, his lavender eyes holding Avery's in a mesmerizing gaze.

"You are *sooo* gorgeous," she replies breathily. He smiles. "Did I just say that out loud? How embarrassing." Avery cringes. The beings laugh gently.

"You're right. He is beautiful." The wedding-dress-model look-alike smiles.

The fiery-orange being clears his throat.

"Yes, you're gorgeous too, Theo." She laughs and squeezes his biceps. "You know I can't get enough of your big muscles."

Avery instantly relaxes in their company, enjoying their light-hearted playfulness. "Are you the insect guardian?" she asks Tate, sensing an intangible closeness to him that she doesn't quite feel with the others.

"Yes, I am. You and I work together to protect all the creatures that live on Earth, and we do our best to shield them from extinction. My inner insect is a bee. So, just like you, I can easily fly almost anywhere without being noticed."

"That's so cool."

"It sure is." He turns to the beautiful woman on his right. "Now, try to guess what Madilyn is responsible for."

"You're the air guardian."

"That's right. I keep an eye on the atmosphere, the wind currents, and the thunderstorms. I work very closely with the Earth guardian."

She points to Theo. "And I guess that's who you are. Right?"

"You've got it. I keep an eye on the land, the minerals, and the volcanoes to ensure all living beings have a safe home."

"Theo and I are the only guardians that never take human form. We never leave this dimension," Madilyn explains. "It's just the two of us. We don't work with a group of protectors like the others, so we can't afford to be distracted from our focus. It's been this way since the Earth's inception."

"Seriously? There are only two of you?"

"That's right," Theo interjects. "But the cool thing is, we are the only two guardians who are completely in synch with all inner beings. We simultaneously learn and grow from all human experiences and can immediately apply the knowledge we acquire to help address urgent ecological concerns."

"My grandma told me we're all connected, but I had no idea what it truly meant, until this very moment."

"Now that we've all introduced ourselves, there's something we'd like to show you," says Tate.

"Please, take our hands to create a circle," adds Madilyn.

The three entities extend their arms and hold hands. They reach out to Avery, and she does the same. An all-encompassing feeling of appreciation floods over her the instant their hands touch. A captivating white light appears in the centre, just as the circle is completed. At that moment, Avery knows she is looking at the entire universe.

The image shifts until the only thing she sees is Earth. As she watches, awestruck, the beautiful blue and green planet turns grey and black. Stunned, she looks at Theo and asks, "What is this?"

"We brought you here tonight to show you what our planet will look like in the future if we don't take immediate action."

The image magnifies, revealing dried up rivers and lakes, leafless trees with broken limbs, and animal skeletons everywhere.

"Please stop!" She cries, instinctively pulling her hands away to cover her eyes. The image abruptly disappears. "What's going on? There's nothing left. All the trees, the plants, the rivers. All the poor insects and animals. Everything's dead."

"If we do nothing, humans will destroy the planet," Madilyn explains. "So many of them only care about making money, and they ignore the consequences of their behaviour. If we don't act soon, Earth will cease to exist."

"I'm sorry these images upset you," Tate continues. "But you must know the truth. As an animal protector, you must do all you can to shield the animals from extinction."

"How am I supposed to do that?"

"You must dedicate your life to finding ways."

Avery repeatedly shakes her head in disbelief.

"Time is running out," Madilyn says seriously. "This is why we've been awaking protectors to their true purpose. We're counting on you—on all awoken protectors. Together, we must convince humans to stop hurting our planet before it's too late. The fate of the world is in our hands."

Overwhelmed, Avery's subconscious leaps back into her human body. At that very moment, she hears her name repeated over and over. She opens her eyes and sees her mother leaning over her. "You were screaming in your sleep. Were you having a nightmare?"

Out of breath, Avery throws her arms around her mother. "It was awful. Our planet was destroyed. All the animals were dead. All of them!"

"Oh, my love. That must have been horrible."

"It really was," she adds as she pulls on her sleeve to wipe the tears and dripping snot from her nose.

"Look around. Everything's fine."

"No! It's not, Mom. You know the planet's in danger. We hear about it every day, and no one's doing anything about it."

"Try to calm down, Ave. It was just a bad dream."

"Yeah, but it felt real. We need to do something. We can't wait. We're all going to die!"

"Sweetie, take a deep breath and try to relax. Follow me. Inhale . . . exhale . . . inhale . . . exhale."

Avery tries her best to follow her mother's lead and finally manages to stop crying. "Please stay with me until I fall back to sleep."

"Of course," replies Isabel. She gently strokes her daughter's hair as Avery lies back down and drifts into an exhausted sleep.

The next morning, Avery lies in bed with her face buried under her pillow.

If we all choose the life we need to live, then why did I pick this one? She sighs loudly. *Last night's dream felt so real, but it can't be true. I can't be responsible for the fate of the animal kingdom. I just can't! I mean . . . I can see what's happening when I visit the other dimension, but there's no way I can do anything here. In real life. I'm just fifteen. How am I supposed to shield animals from extinction or convince humans to stop hurting our planet? I can't even help the animals at the zoo. What are they thinking?*

Feeling hopeless, Avery weeps heavy tears.

I don't care what Grandpa said. This is too much for me! I don't want to follow my calling. I just want to go to soccer practise and hangout with my friends. I want my old life back. I just want to be a regular teenager!

CHAPTER 24

THE FOLLOWING FRIDAY, Avery drags herself to school—again. She hasn't been able to focus all week. To make things worse, Jake is away at a swim competition, and she doesn't feel like talking with anyone else.

"Hey, there you are." Paige bounces up and gives Avery a hug. "I've been looking for you all morning. Are you avoiding me?"

"No, nothing like that." She regrets not being able to hide her feelings any better.

Paige cocks her head to one side and looks Avery straight in the eye. "You know I'm always here for you. Let's hang out after school."

"Okay," Avery half-heartedly agrees, more out of guilt than desire.

When the last school bell of the day rings, Paige and Avery grab their backpacks and make their way to their childhood hangout—the neighbourhood park where they used to play.

"Paige, do you hear that? There's something wrong."

"What do you mean? The only thing I hear are birds singing."

"Don't you hear? They're not singing. They're screaming!" Avery drops her backpack and darts toward the tree where the loud chirping is coming from. There is movement in the bushes under it. She leans in and pulls out a baby rabbit twisted up in the handle of an old plastic bag. "Paige, look in my bag. I think I have a pair of scissors in my pencil case."

"Found them! What should I do?"

She points to the spots that need attention. "Cut the handle right here. Good. And now here. Okay, one last cut should do it. Right here." She gently pulls the pieces apart and frees the small mammal, who looks in every direction and quickly hops away.

"That was amazing. I can't believe you saved another animal!" Paige gazes at her friend with pride, but instead of looking happy, Avery's expression is troubled.

"There's something I need to tell you, and it's sort of related to this."

Paige points to the nearest park bench. "You want to sit down? This looks like it might be kind of serious."

The girls take a seat on the bench. Avery kicks at the small stones scattered on the ground in front of them.

"I'm glad I could save the rabbit, but what real power do I have? None. That's the answer. NONE!" Her eyes glisten.

"I don't know what you mean," Paige frowns. "What power?"

Avery looks at her friend anxiously.

"You know you can trust me, Ave," Paige reassures her. "We've been best friends forever."

Paige's kind expression helps Avery decide to share with her friend. She tells Paige about the zoo, and her fears for the animals. She describes her dreams and talks about her past lives, explaining that she is an animal protector. Paige listens in silence until Avery tells her she can shapeshift into a falcon.

"A falcon?" she looks at Avery quizzically.

"Yes. Last night, my friend, Theo, the Earth guardian, told me that a fire was starting in Southern California, so I warned the animals to avoid the area that was going to be engulfed in flames. A few days ago, I flew over the Atlantic Ocean and redirected a pod of whales that was headed for a massive oil spill. And last week, when we learned about the Amazon Rainforest, I went there when I went to bed that night and helped a family of spider monkeys avoid getting shot by poachers."

"I'd love to have dreams like that. It must be like watching a movie every night."

Avery shakes her head rapidly. "These aren't dreams. These are real experiences. I told you—I've been visiting another dimension."

"Come on, Ave," Paige replies, unconvinced.

"Paige, please. I need you to believe me. You're my best friend. I wouldn't lie to you." Avery tears up.

"Okay. Whatever. I believe you," says Paige, grabbing her phone. She adds, "Sorry, Ave, I have to head home."

Paige gets up and walks away without saying another word.

Shoot! I knew I shouldn't have said anything. Avery feels sick to her stomach and can't face her shift at the zoo. She heads home and asks her mother to call in sick for her, before burying herself under the bed covers.

CHAPTER 25

ON MONDAY MORNING, Avery's feeling better. She realized over the weekend that she probably overreacted to Paige's abrupt departure on Friday. She's looking forward to seeing her best friend so they can catch up. As she approaches her locker, she sees a pink sticky note with messy writing scrawled across the paper. It says *FREAK!!*

She pulls the note off and crumples it in her hand. *Thank goodness no one's around. That's so mean. Who would do such a thing?* She opens her locker, picks up her books and laptop, and heads to class—five minutes early. As usual.

Avery enters the science lab. She sees Paige chatting with one of their classmates, Crissy, who quiets down as soon as she notices Avery enter the room.

That's weird. She awkwardly waves *hello* as she makes her way to her desk—neither respond. *Shoot! What's happening?*

She lays her bag on her desk and aims for the front of the room to feed Bruno and Baxter—a pair of lab rats Ms. Bello rescued a few months ago—which is, by far, the best part of science class.

Trying to ease her anxiety, Avery grabs Bruno, gently pets him, and whispers to Baxter, "Don't worry, buddy, you're next—"

Avery stops what she's doing and tries to focus on a faraway conversation. *Is Paige talking about me? What is she—*

Interrupting Avery's thoughts, Crissy mutters, "There she goes again. Saving the world, one rodent at a time."

Dumbfounded, Avery mindlessly puts the rat back in its cage as she hears her own voice rage in her head. *How could Paige betray me like that? She told Crissy! I thought we were friends . . . best friends.*

"Paige! How could you?"

Avery grabs her bag and storms out of the classroom as she hears Paige's voice say, "Chill out, Ave. Crissy was only joking."

Avery is completely flustered. Her eyes glisten with tears as she sprints to her locker.

Don't cry. Don't cry. You can't let anyone see you're hurt.

She's so focused on holding back her tears that she literally runs into her science teacher. "Avery, watch where you're going. You almost made me drop these folders."

"Sorry, Mrs. Bello. I didn't see you."

"That's pretty obvious. Isn't it?"

"Sorry . . ." Avery holds back tears.

"Are you okay?"

"Yeah . . . I just forgot something in my locker."

"Okay, then. But hurry up!"

"Will do," Avery answers as they both walk away.

"Oh! Avery!"

She stops and turns back. "Yes, Mrs. Bello?"

"Did you feed Bruno and Baxter this morning?"

"No, I didn't get a chance to."

"Okay, I'll do it before starting class. Hurry back now!"

"Sure thing, Mrs. Bello," responds Avery, who makes her way to the closest washroom, enters a stall, locks the door, and starts balling.

This is so unfair. I can't believe Paige did this. I thought I could trust her.

Why is this happening to me? Why is my life so hard? What am I going to tell Jake? Oh, no . . . what if he's already heard? He's definitely going to dump me.

Starting to panic, Avery feels her heart pound in her chest. She looks around and sees stars, then darkness. She passes out, hitting the floor hard as she falls.

CHAPTER 26

AVERY COMES ROUND just as Jake walks into the nurse's office. He rushes over to the bed to help her sit up. "What happened? I came as soon as I heard you were here."

"I don't know. I felt woozy, and then everything was black."

"How did I get here?"

The nurse replies, "Tom, the janitor, found you passed out in the girls' washroom." She continues, "I'm sure you'll be fine. Your vitals are completely normal. A lot of students are overtired this time of year. Your mom should be here soon."

Avery nods in acknowledgement. She sees Jake talking, but she doesn't hear a word.

Why's he being so nice? I guess the rumour mill hasn't made it to him, yet.

"Babe. What's up? You're breathing super hard."

"Really?! I didn't notice." *Jake's so sweet. I have to do everything I can to make sure he doesn't break up with me over this—*

Avery's thoughts are interrupted by her mother rushing into the nurse's office.

"I was so worried about you. I must have run four red lights to get here. Are you okay? I knew you didn't look ready to go back to school this morning."

"It's okay. I'm sure I'll be fine. Can we go home?"

Jake awkwardly leans over to give his girlfriend a kiss before Isabel helps her to her feet and walks her to the car—students staring and whispering as they see her leave.

Avery spends the rest of the day sobbing in bed. Every time she looks at her phone—it's radio silence.

Emotionally destroyed, Avery switches off her phone and spends the remainder of the day in bed with the lights off.

The next morning, she awakes feeling devastated.

I can't face them. I just can't.

"Mom, can you come here, please," Avery calls, unable to keep the despair out of her voice.

Isabel quietly opens her daughter's bedroom door and perches on the edge of her bed. "What's wrong, my love? Are you still feeling under the weather?" She gently puts the back of her hand against Avery's forehead and cheeks. "You don't feel warm, but you still look exhausted. Did you manage to sleep?"

"I did, but I don't want to go to school today." Avery leans against her mother's shoulder as tears cover her face.

"You don't have to go," Isabel soothes.

"Thanks, Mom." Avery lets go, turns to face the wall, snuggles against Shadow, and pulls the covers over her head to hide from the world.

Isabel makes her way to the kitchen. Teagan has just piled a spoonful of cereal into her mouth, and she stuffs her cheeks like a hamster, incoherently asking her mom what's going on.

"Is Ave missing school again? I guess yesterday really freaked her out."

"What do you mean?"

"Paige's sister told me they had a fight. I don't know what it was about, but from what I heard, some of the other students got involved and Ave was so stressed that she passed out. I hope she'll be okay."

"Thanks, love. That's helpful. I'll let her rest for now and speak with her in a bit. Finish your breakfast, and then Eric will drop you off at school."

Teagan nods vigorously as she stuffs another spoonful of cereal into her mouth.

CHAPTER 27

A COUPLE OF HOURS LATER, Isabel softly knocks on her daughter's bedroom door. "May I come in?"

"Sure," Avery replies quietly, gently stroking Shadow's fluffy back. He purrs loudly. *At least Shadow still loves me.*

"How are you feeling? Any better?"

"Sort of, I guess."

"Would you like a warm bowl of butternut squash soup?"

"You made my favourite? Thanks, Mom." She tries her best to smile.

She leans her face into Shadow's belly—igniting his instinct to gently massage Avery's forehead while increasing his powerful purr. *I love you too, sweetie. I don't know what I would do without you. Don't ever leave me, my little ball of love.*

A few minutes later, Isabel enters the room holding a wooden tray with a bowl of soup, crackers, cubes of marble cheese, and a tall glass of ice water.

"You're the best. Thanks, Mom." Avery sits up and takes the tray, making a mini sandwich with the cheese and crackers. Her mother tidies up the room.

"I had no idea I was actually hungry," Avery says after swallowing the last mouthful of soup.

Isabel places the tray on the floor before sitting on Avery's bed and looking at her daughter with a mixture of love and concern.

"Ave, I'd like to talk with you for a minute."

Oh, no! What does she want now? Avery nods, silent. Her heart sinks. "Mom, I don't want to talk. Thanks for the food, but can you please leave my room?" says Avery, not sure how much more anxiety she can take.

"Avery, don't be rude! You don't even know what I'm about to say."

She sighs loudly, lying back down and pulling the covers over her head. *Aaarrrggg! Do we really have to do this? Just leave me alone . . . leave!*

Ignoring her daughter's behaviour, Isabel states, "Teagan told me you had a fight with Paige. Is that true?"

Avery immediately pulls the cover off and sits up.

"How did she hear about that? We don't even go to the same school. Does everybody know? This is horrible!"

"She heard from Paige's sister. What was the fight about?"

"It was nothing. Don't worry about it."

"It's obviously something, given the way you just reacted. Please, my love, tell me what's going on. I want to help you."

"I told Paige a secret in confidence, and she told Crissy. And I'm pretty sure Crissy told everyone!"

"I'm sure that's not true."

"Oh, yeah? Well, look at this." She grabs her phone, powers it on, and shows her mother Paige's blocked social media pages. "She's cutting me out! All because of . . . well, it doesn't matter. Paige isn't who I thought she was."

"Oh, darling. Come here." Isabel leans in to hold her child in her arms. "I'm sure you and Paige can fix this. You've been best friends for a very long time."

"No! It's too late. And now, everybody hates me." Avery whimpers.

"What do you mean, *everybody hates you*?" asks Isabel as she hands Avery a box of tissues.

She grabs a tissue, blows her nose, and says, "Normally, when I miss school, I get a ton of messages—" Avery can't finish her sentence.

"Yes, go on, love."

"And I haven't received a single one—not one! Not even from Jake!"

"Oh, dear. That must be awful being snubbed like that," Isabel reassures her, trying to come up with a plan to help salvage the situation.

"I'm so embarrassed. I can't go back to school—ever!"

"Hold on, Ave. Let's try to figure this out."

Avery scoots down and stares at her hands.

"You need to show your classmates that you're tough. That no one can rattle you. That no one can push you around. You must use your words and convince them that no matter what they say—or don't say—it doesn't affect you."

"But, Mom, I passed out at school. How can I convince them that Paige's betrayal didn't affect me?"

"Just tell them you were sick, and it had nothing to do with what Paige told Crissy."

"Yeah, but—" Avery stops mid-sentence and shrugs.

"You just have to pretend that you have no idea what Crissy was talking about. Or pretend that what she said didn't bother you."

"That won't work."

"Trust me. It will."

"No one will believe me."

"If your story is credible and well delivered, they will. I faced a similar situation when I was about your age, and this is how I managed to get through it."

"But, Mom, are you seriously suggesting that I lie? You've always told me how important it is to tell the truth."

"Look at it this way. Is it an option, for you, to stop going to school?"

"No." She sighs loudly.

"So, you'll need to figure out a way to get over this situation. Or pretend like what happened no longer bothers you. Right?"

"I guess."

"So, telling your classmates that what Crissy said didn't bother you and that you passed out for medical reasons isn't really a lie. Is it?"

"I guess not—if you put it that way." Avery exhales loudly. "Okay," she says, "I'll try to figure out exactly what to say."

CHAPTER 28

AVERY AWAKES WITH CONVICTION. *Today, I'm taking control of my life.*

Isabel appears in the kitchen as Avery's almost done with her breakfast. "You're up early? *Aaahhh*, and you made coffee. Isn't that nice?" She pours herself a hot cup of morning comfort. "You must be feeling better."

"Yup, I slept well, and I feel ready. I'm a bit nervous, but I know I can do it."

"I'm really happy to hear that."

Avery gets up, gives her mother a hug, and heads off to school with her head held high. No matter what happens, nothing will stop her from going through with her plan.

When she gets close to her locker, she sees Jake. It's clear that he's waiting for her. Feeling as though she may throw up, she tries to calm down.

Keep your cool. Stick to the plan. It'll be fine.

"Hey, babe. You're back. I wasn't sure if you'd make it to school today."

She looks at him, confused. *Why's he being so nice? What's up with—*

"Sorry I didn't text you. My dad took my phone because I failed my math test." Jake leans in for a hug.

Phew! What a relief! She smiles.

"No worries. I didn't have my phone either. My mom took mine so I could rest."

Avery feels horrible about lying to him, but she can't face telling him about being shunned by everyone." *I'll tell him later—not now.* Her thoughts are interrupted by the bell. They grab their things and head to their respective classrooms.

"Have fun in science class. See you later." Jake lifts her hand to kiss it goodbye.

"You're so cheesy." She smiles. The corny gesture was exactly what she needed to get back into the right headspace to go through with the plan.

As she pushes the door open, the bubble of chatting teenagers turns into sniggering. Mrs. Bello's running late, and Avery is pleased about that. She walks to her desk, but instead of sitting down in shame, she whacks her books on the table. The room instantly drops into silence. Avery doesn't miss a beat and jumps right into her well-prepared speech.

"You guys are such followers."

The entire class is dumbstruck.

"You heard a rumour about me, and you saw that Paige and Crissy blocked me from their accounts, so you did the same. Seriously? I've known most of you since kindergarten. Don't you think that's worth something? I passed out at school—for crying out loud! Couldn't you have taken a few minutes to see how I was doing and get my side of the story, instead of simply following the crowd?"

Paige stands up to speak just as Mrs. Bello steps into class and tells everyone to take their seats.

Avery sits down and quickly scans the room. No one is looking at her. They're all giving Paige and Crissy the stink eye. Paige's face is flushed with embarrassment, and Avery knows her former best friend well enough to tell that she is doing her best not to cry.

I did it! Mom was right. It worked!

At the end of class, Avery proudly walks out of the room, acting as though nothing had ever happened.

Everything's okay. Everything's okay.

Avery silently repeats the mantra over and over to keep her emotions in check.

"Hey, Avery, wait up," shouts one of her classmates. "I can't believe I got dragged into that stuff Crissy was spreading around. She's got a mind like a five-year-old. So uncool. Anyhow, forgive and forget?"

Avery nods and smiles. "Sure thing. We all make mistakes."

She walks away, heading toward her locker, ignoring Paige who is calling after her, "Ave, wait up. Let's talk, please!"

Avery picks up the books for her next class and heads down the corridor, away from her former best friend. Undeterred, Paige bombards Avery with texts. After ignoring at least two dozen messages, Avery decides to reply. Keeping in mind that Paige could easily forward her text to everyone, she carefully considers her response: "*You broke my heart. I thought we were best friends. Stop texting me. I don't ever want to talk to you again.*"

Avery's eyes tear up when she hears the swoosh of the text being sent. She has never felt so betrayed. She didn't even know these feelings were possible.

Wanting to put all of this behind her, Avery decides to tell Jake part of the story over lunch. She tells him that Paige misinterpreted something she said last Friday and betrayed her confidence by telling Crissy, who blabbed to everyone and used it to turn her classmates against her. "I'm sorry I didn't talk to you about it before. I just needed to deal with this on my own."

"I get it, babe. It's okay. I never liked those two anyway." He winks and gives her an elbow nudge.

After school, Avery walks home feeling extremely relieved.

That was so hard. Why can't my life be simpler? The visions, the bullying, the freaky things happening at the zoo. I can't deal with this anymore. Maybe when I'm older, I'll be able to focus on my life's purpose, but this is too much for me right now. Avery sighs loudly as she repeatedly shakes her head. *I don't want to keep moving between dimensions. I need to find a way to get my old life back.*

She cuts through the park and sits for a while, thinking about what to do.

I was strong enough to stop the bullying. I should be able to stop everything else that's been happening. Right?!

She closes her eyes, lifts her head, and whispers, "Grandma, I'm asking for your help. I'm not ready. I can't take it. Please find a way to help the animals at the zoo without me. Work with the other protectors and do something to help them, but don't involve me. I don't want this anymore. I don't want to visit the parallel universe anymore. I love you very much and I'll miss being with you, but please help me get my old life back. Please!"

CHAPTER 29

A FEW DAYS PASS. Nothing. A few weeks go by—still nothing. Avery is now convinced—her paranormal experiences were a result of her overactive imagination. She's finally able to put those thoughts behind her.

Things are back to normal at school, other than her friendship with Paige. Avery still feels betrayed and knows that, if she hadn't been able to convince her classmates that Paige had got it wrong, the bullying could have dragged on for a lot longer. Life at home is back to the same familiar routines that she sometimes used to find dull, but now she feels grateful for any semblance of normal.

The minute their daily chores are over, Avery and Teagan run outside to play basketball in the backyard. Isabel, who is finishing up in the kitchen, hears distressed gasps from the mudroom. Worried, she heads in that direction and yelps, "Eric, come quick! Daisy's choking."

"Does she have something in her mouth?"

"I don't know," Isabel hesitantly says, trying her best to look. "She doesn't seem to have anything. Quick, do something! Call 9-1-1!"

"9-1-1 isn't for animals. They won't come here for that. Will they?"

"I don't know, but we need to do something!"

"What's going on?" Teagan says, entering through the patio door with Avery, both worried by their parents' panicked screams.

"Daisy's choking, and we don't know what to do."

"I can help!" Avery darts toward Daisy. "I learned animal first aid when I started at the zoo. Did you check her mouth? Is there anything stuck?"

"I don't think so. I didn't see anything."

"Eric, lift her back legs while I check her mouth."

"There's nothing. Bring her legs down," says Avery, moving positions and starting the Heimlich maneuver. She gives a few upward pushes, and a large, orange sponge is expelled from her mouth.

"Thank goodness," says Isabel. She's relieved for a moment, until she realizes something. "Why isn't she waking up?"

"There may be other pieces," says Eric, opening Daisy's mouth while Avery looks inside. "Or maybe she stopped breathing too long and needs CPR."

"I know how to do that too! Eric, lay her on her side. Mom, put your fingers here." Avery directs her mother's hand to Daisy's inner thigh. "And let me know if you feel her pulse. Eric, be ready to press her chest near her armpit, and I'll blow puffs of air into her nose."

Avery and Eric start CPR and work in concert as though they've done this before. Avery's in complete control, even though she's worried sick.

"I feel Daisy's pulse," Isabel says.

"And I just felt her exhale," Avery adds. Everybody stops moving and stares at the poor old dog.

"I just saw her chest move," exclaims Teagan. "There it goes again!"

Avery lays her head on Daisy, places her hand near her dog's muzzle, and starts crying the instant she feels Daisy's chest move up and down.

CHAPTER 30

A FEW HOURS LATER, Avery goes to bed feeling exhausted from the overwhelmingly emotional experience—grateful for having been able to save her dog. But she wonders if this incident is somehow linked to her 'supposed' paranormal powers.

No, it can't be. I haven't had a dream in weeks. None of it is possible. I'm just a regular teenager with an overactive imagination. I made the whole thing up. I know I did!

Trying to convince herself, Avery drifts into sleep. She finds herself standing in the blackness of space, surrounded by countless stars and colourful faraway nebulae.

No. Not this again!

"I don't want these dreams anymore. Please, somebody help me!"

"Sweetie." Avery hears a familiar voice and turns around to see Kamila standing beside her. "This is your fate. You can't run away from it."

"But Grandma, I just want to have a normal life. It's too much for me to handle."

"Avery, you were born to help animals. You can't deny it, no matter how hard you try. You even proved it tonight when you saved Daisy."

"Anyone with training would have been able to do that, even if they weren't an animal protector."

"You may be right, but I'm not so sure someone else would've had the instinct to know exactly what to do, how, and when. You must find a way to live with this new reality. We need you. We won't be able to save the planet if you don't help us. Trust me, things will get easier. I promise." Kamila hugs her beloved granddaughter, who sobs in her arms.

"I tried so hard to convince myself that none of this is real. I don't know what to do. It feels like so much responsibility."

"You are so brave. Trust yourself. You have the answers—you just need to ask yourself the right questions." Kamila smiles, kisses Avery's forehead, then vanishes.

Avery stands alone in the black, endless space. She sees a beautiful blue light and walks toward it. Hundreds of tall beings, dressed in different shades of blue, appear out of nowhere. Although none of them are speaking, Avery can clearly interpret their thoughts. They are all linked. So, even though she can't pinpoint which thought is coming from which being, everything makes sense.

One by one, the beings turn and look in her direction. She feels heat building in her body. She moves closer to them. One reaches his hand out to Avery, and she instinctively does the same to the being next to her, who reaches out to the next being, and so on, until they create an enormous circle. The instant the ring closes, a luminescent globe appears in the middle. It is covered by millions of thin blue light beams that continually appear and disappear.

Fascinated and intrigued, Avery watches in awe, until she feels a light tap on her shoulder. She turns her head and discovers two elegant beings standing beside her. The first is dressed in red, and the second, in green. She gently releases her grip from the circle.

CHAPTER 31

"ZANDER! I HAVEN'T SEEN YOU in forever! I'm so happy to see you again!"

"Me too," he replies with genuine enthusiasm. "Let me introduce you to my friend, Willow."

"I'm pleased to meet you," responds the beautiful being dressed in a ruby-red ballgown, with dark-cherry eyes that are emphasized by her thick, scarlet-red hair. "Your grandmother told us you'd be here today."

"Hmm . . . I should have known this was her doing." Avery smiles at her two companions.

"You know how persistent your grandmother can be," replies Zander, winking at Avery, who rolls her eyes, smiles, and laughs. "I hope you're in the mood to learn. We have a ton of information for you."

"If I can't stop my destiny, I might as well learn as much as I can," she agrees.

"Fantastic. Follow us," adds Willow. They make their way deeper into the parallel universe, seeing countless circles of beings just like the one Avery was part of a moment ago.

Each group encloses its own translucent sphere. The millions of light beams that encase the globes match the colour of the entities that contain it. Together, they create a rainbow of harmonic bubbles.

"Isn't it wonderful to see all these protectors working together to sustain life?" asks Willow.

"What do you mean, 'to sustain life'?"

"Each beam of light represents a life form that comes to Earth, lives, and dies," replies Willow. "The blue ones represent animals, the red lights are humans, the purple are insects, and the green ones are trees, plants, and vegetation. And, like your grandmother previously explained, since time doesn't exist, these protectors are here with us right now, but many of them are also on Earth living their human experiences."

"I still have a hard time wrapping my head around that concept."

"Watch." Willow smiles and waves her hands, magically transforming the landscape into a sunset savannah.

"Whoa, that was awesome!" Avery looks in every direction and spots a few random acacia trees in the distance, a small herd of elephants, and a few giraffes.

"She likes to show off sometimes," snickers Zander.

Willow winks and smiles as she pokes Zander's shoulder. "As I was saying," she continues, "your inner consciousness is here with us right now, and it is also in your human body resting in your bed. But, if you chose to, your inner being could also be standing with your fellow animal protectors in the circle you helped form earlier, or creating a river of love-filled water to nourish the planet's inner core, or soaring through the sky after shapeshifting into its inner animal."

"All at the same time?"

"Yep, and that's not all," adds Zander. "Your inner consciousness is always looking after animals, no matter what you're doing on Earth."

"Seriously? Even when I have no idea?"

"That's right."

"That's amazing!"

"Have you noticed anything weird since you started to visit this alternate universe?"

"Did he seriously just ask me that?" Avery looks directly at Willow, as they both laugh out loud.

"Okay, okay. Let me rephrase," says Zander, laughing as well. "Have you ever noticed tiny dots of blue, yellow, or white lights that flash in the blink of an eye?"

"Yes, actually. I just thought my eyes were acting up."

"Okay, what about this? Have you ever felt an odd, tingling sensation on the back of your scalp?"

"Yes, I have. It feels so weird. I thought a bug was walking on my head. The other day, I actually asked my mom to check if I had lice. You should have seen the panic on her face. Poor thing."

"These mystic 'winks' remind us of our true mission, and that our inner consciousness is hard at work in this dimension even when we're busy focusing on our daily activities," says Zander. "To be honest, life gets in the way sometimes. I get busy and I forget about my calling. But then, out of nowhere, I feel the gentle tingle at the back of my head, or I notice a flash of light in the corner of my eye, and it unfailingly brings me back to this place. And I love it. It reminds me of my bigger purpose, and it makes me feel wonderful."

"I'll try to remember that next time it feels like I have bugs dancing on my head." Avery laughs.

CHAPTER 32

"THERE'S SOMETHING ELSE you might find interesting—about the dots of light that flash before your eyes," Willow says.

"What's that?"

"Each time you see one, it means that a human protector paid you a visit."

"Umm . . . that's kind of creepy."

"It definitely would be if human protectors could shapeshift into different humans like you shapeshift into a falcon," Zander laughs.

"But let me reassure you—that's not the case," adds Willow.

"Phew! Because that would definitely freak me out!" All three beings laugh out loud.

"Do you remember how your grandmother explained that this dimension vibrates at a different frequency than the one on Earth?"

"Yes, she said that this parallel universe exists at a wavelength that humans can't see. Just like I can't see how my phone sends or receives texts and pictures."

"That's right," Zander confirms. "And the only individuals who can access both dimensions are awoken protectors, like you, or guardians, like us."

"And that's pretty much how human protectors keep an eye on humanity," Willow continues. "We follow our heart, pretty much the same way you open yours when you want to shapeshift. The main difference is that we don't choose where to go; we let our heart guide us to those who need us. We stay in this dimension and visit individuals without disturbing them. We can see what they're up to, but only if their inner being lets us. This is our failsafe to ensure we never invade anyone's privacy."

"That's amazing . . ."

"And she can do even more."

"Get out! You have more than one superpower?"

"Yes, I have two. I also possess the innate power of persuasion."

"Being persuasive isn't a superpower, is it?"

"It is for human protectors. We are expert communicators. We are pure-hearted, creative, inventive, and outspoken. We use our words and actions to convey positivity and influence humans to think about others and to do their part to save the world."

"I don't want to sound negative," Avery chimes in, "but are you sure this is working? My stepdad watches the news every night, and it doesn't seem as though many humans are thinking about others."

"That's true," replies Zander. "Regrettably, we rarely hear stories of kind-hearted people and their endeavours, but with our plan of action—and the fact that all protectors have now been awoken to their innate calling—we will be hard to ignore."

"Especially since human protectors represent the vast majority of protectors," interjects Willow.

"You do?" curiously asks Avery.

"Yes," replies Willow. "In fact, there's at least one human protector in every country, and depending on the country's size and population density, there can be up to several hundred of us."

"How many are there in total?"

"There are about seventy-five hundred human protectors," answers Zander. "That's huge compared to the meagre two hundred fifty plant protectors."

"Whoa! That's quite the difference. How many animal protectors are there?"

"One thousand," replies Zander. "Let me break it down for you. Out of the ten thousand protectors, seventy-five hundred are *human*, one thousand are *animal*, one thousand are *insect*, two hundred fifty are *plant*, and two hundred fifty are *water*. And none are *Earth* or *air*."

"Oh, yeah! That's right," jumps in Avery. "Theo and Madilyn mentioned that they don't work with protectors."

He nods in agreement.

"What about you, Zander? What's your superpower? Can you shapeshift or visit plants and trees whenever you want?"

"Not exactly, but I can communicate with them."

"For real?"

"Yes, we can send messages to all types of vegetation by using a unique harmonic frequency that reaches their roots. For example, plant protectors can warn vegetation when a wildfire is approaching, or when a hurricane is coming, or when bulldozers are heading their way."

"Sorry, but what's the point in warning them if they can't do anything to save themselves? I mean, trees and plants can't run or fly away like animals or insects do."

"That's a valid point, but because we know when a forest will be devastated by an upcoming fire, for instance, we can tell the trees to use their roots to soak up as much water as possible, to help their trunk and branches resist the flames. While this is happening, we release an invisible magical shield that insulates their roots and their recently fallen cones and fruits. Once the fire is over, many of these can be found safely buried under ash and soot until it is safe for them to grow back, which is typically several years after an incident."

"That's incredible."

"It truly is. Ever since I've been awoken to my true purpose, I experience an inexplicable feeling when I'm in the middle of a forest and surrounded by trees. It's as though I become one with them. I can't imagine anything better than being the plant guardian."

CHAPTER 33

"WILLOW AND I have one more thing to show you tonight." Zander waves his hands and scenes of different places on Earth are projected into the air. "We want to give you a sneak peek of the future—to show you what our planet will look like two decades from now if all the awoken protectors do their best to accomplish their true purpose."

"As you can see, greenhouse gas levels will significantly decrease, because major car manufacturers will finally agree to only produce zero-emission vehicles. Also, all commercial planes and cargo ships will be solely powered by biofuel."

Willow points to several images of the Pacific Ocean. "And the plastic garbage islands that came to life in the 1990s will finally be cleared up."

"That's unbelievable!"

"Look at all of these self-sustaining manufacturing plants that will pop up in Africa." Zander points to the images of flourishing African countries.

"Indeed," adds Willow. "Several large international companies will partner to help the poorest parts of the world thrive. They will create jobs and training opportunities for local people. And they will provide power to smaller businesses and surrounding communities by capturing and redistributing one hundred percent of the energy their manufacturing plants produce."

"We'll also see many eco-friendly inventions finally become available to the general consumer. Just like these windmills," Zander continues. "All these houses will be self-sustained by wind, and these houses over here will be solely powered by the sun."

"This is so exciting," says Avery, as Willow gently waves her hands and erases the images. "I can't believe all of these changes will happen so soon. I guess small individual acts can actually have a real impact."

"Yes, they can. And remember, you're not the only one we've reached out to. There are over ten thousand protectors. We've been in contact with all of them, and our hope is that they'll all play their part."

"It's not a simple task, but it is achievable," adds Zander. "It's the strength of our collective efforts that will make a real difference. And now that you know so much about this alternate universe, and all the powers that lie within, it's up to you to figure out what you'll do with that information, and what role you'll play to help save our beautiful planet."

CHAPTER 34

THE NEXT MORNING, Avery wakes up with Daisy resting on her bed.

"How are you feeling this morning?" Avery lifts Daisy's head and gives her at least twenty kisses. With their nose and snout gently pressed together, Avery looks straight into her dog's big, brown eyes. "I didn't even hear you come into my room last night. I love you so much, girl." Daisy looks at Avery, licks her twice on the chin, and lies back down to continue sleeping.

Teagan barges through Avery's bedroom door saying, "There you are! I've been looking everywhere for you." Teagan leans in and hugs her beloved dog. "You scared me last night. Don't you ever do that again." Daisy lifts her head, looks into Teagan's teary eyes, licks her salty cheek, and lies back down, closing her eyes.

"Morning, ladies," says Eric, making his way up the stairs from the kitchen. "I spoke with the vet this morning and told him about last night. He asked us to keep an eye on Daisy, but she should be perfectly fine. He also said that we were incredibly lucky given her age. She probably would have died if we hadn't performed the Heimlich and CPR. It's all because of you, Avery. You saved Daisy's life!"

"Thank you so much," exclaims Teagan, jumping into her big sister's arms.

"Oh! And I've made a special breakfast to celebrate the beginning of summer break. Come downstairs before it gets cold."

"Thanks, Eric. I'll be there in a few minutes. I just want to sit with Daisy for a bit," Avery says.

Teagan runs down the stairs.

Avery sits on her bed and lovingly pets her resting dog. *There's no way I can deny it anymore. I'm an animal protector, and I must find a way to live my life's purpose. I need to team up with Sky and figure out a way to stop what's happening at the zoo.*

Later that morning, as Avery cycles through her neighbourhood, she sees Pike across the street, cycling in the other direction. "Hey, Pike. How's it going?" She drags her feet to slow down.

Feeling flustered like he always does when Avery talks to him, Pike puts his brakes on so fast that he almost flips over his handlebars. He shouts back, "Oh . . . umm . . . hi, Ave! What are the odds of bumping into you?"

"Pretty solid, actually. I live just up the street. Remember?"

"Oh, yeah, that's right." Pike's unnecessarily trying to hide that he knows exactly where she lives. He's been riding his bike in her neighbourhood every day after school for the past two weeks, and several times a day over the weekends, hoping to bump into her. "Where are you headed?"

"Nowhere, really. You?"

"I was heading to the library. There's a book I've been waiting to borrow, and it's finally back. Do you want to tag along?"

"Sure. I haven't been to the library in years. Give me a sec. I'll text my mom so she knows where I'm going."

As they cycle to the library, Pike says, "Ave, there's something I've been meaning to tell you. Do you mind if we stop for a minute?"

"Sure," Avery agrees. "We can go through the park and stop there. It's not much of a detour from the library."

"Great," Pike replies. They pedal in silence for a few minutes until they reach the park. Pike stops at the first bench they come to and waits until they are both settled on the wooden seat.

"What's on your mind, Pike?" Avery asks kindly. She can see something is troubling her friend.

"So . . . you remember when we worked on the English essay, you told me that we pick our life to learn lessons that help our subconscious grow?"

She silently nods in agreement. *Where's he going with this?*

"Well, I started to work on a graphic novel, and I was wondering if you'd give me permission to use some of your ideas in my book."

"Seriously? That's so cool!"

"You really think so?"

"Of course, I do! Oh, and yes, I officially give you permission to use my ideas in your story. Do you have anything to show me?"

"Actually, I do," he replies, grabbing a folder from his backpack that he had hung on his bike handles. "Okay, so before I show you anything, you need to know that these are just rough sketches, and I haven't put much thought on the actual plot yet. I've just started to draw out some of the main scenes and characters."

"Okay, enough with the suspense. Show me!" She enthusiastically states.

He hands her the folder. She opens it, and he starts pacing, feeling extremely vulnerable.

"Gee . . . chill out, Pike." She laughs. "I'm sure I'll love your drawings."

The first illustration depicts a few people standing in a circle surrounding a bright ball. The second shows two people standing on the moon. The third features seven people, each dressed in a different colour— white, orange, green, blue, purple, turquoise, and red.

What is this? These people look like guardians. This one—Avery focuses on the turquoise being—*even looks like Grandma.*

She quickly skims over the rest and blurts out, "How the heck did you come up with these drawings?"

"Why? Don't you like them?"

"No, that's not it. Umm . . . they're just very specific. It's as if you've actually seen these people before."

"Umm . . . no. I mean, I don't know."

Skeptical, she persists, "So, did you, or didn't you, copy these drawings from somewhere?"

"Are you accusing me of stealing copyright?" He crosses his arms, feeling interrogated.

"No, nothing like that. I'm just wondering where you found your inspiration from."

"Oh, okay." He relaxes, sits back down, and adds, "Umm . . . from a movie."

"Yeah, which one?"

"Umm . . . it was actually from a few movies, I think. I can't remember."

"Come on, Pike. I know you can't lie, especially not to me. Just tell me."

"Stop pushing me, Ave." Pike takes a deep breath and blurts out, "I've been visiting a parallel dimension in my dreams. Okay?!"

CHAPTER 35

"SERIOUSLY?" ASKS AVERY.

"You think I'm nuts. Don't you?"

"No, actually. I don't. I can relate . . . a lot!"

"What do you mean?"

"I've also been having dreams where I visit another dimension . . ." replies Avery.

"Hold up! Are you saying that the rumours about you that were circulating in school a few weeks ago . . . were true?"

She nods in agreement.

Dumbfounded, Pike speechlessly stares at Avery who adds, "And when I visit this parallel universe, I morph into my inner being."

"SERIOUSLY! Me too!"

"You do?" Avery impulsively jumps into Pike's arms, then immediately pulls away. *OMG! How embarrassing.* "Sorry, I couldn't help myself."

"That's okay." Pike clears his throat, trying to deal with the fact that the love of his life just threw her arms around him.

Desperate to break the awkward mood, Avery asks, "What does your inner being look like?"

"Hmm . . . I think I'm about twenty years old and I'm dressed in red. What about you? What do you look like?"

"I have dark hair and teal-coloured eyes, and I wear this amazing blue dress. Honestly, I look like a fairy princess ready for prom."

"Wow! I hope I get to see your inner being one day."

"That would be so cool," she exhales deeply.

"I can't believe we're actually openly talking about our inner beings and our experiences in a parallel universe. This whole thing is mind-blowing."

"You're right. This is a pretty strange conversation." Avery smiles and winks at her new best friend.

"I had a feeling you'd understand, but I never would've guessed that we were in the same boat."

"I know. What are the odds? Anyway, I'm really happy to be friends with another awoken protector."

"What do you mean by 'awoken protector'?"

"Hold on . . . you don't know that you're an awoken human protector?"

"I'm a what, now?"

"I'm shocked no one's told you about this."

Pike shrugs his shoulders.

"I'm an animal protector—we're all dressed in blue. You're a human protector—you guys are dressed in red."

"For real?"

"Yeah! Hold on. How many dreams have you had?"

"Four."

"That's weird. I was told I was an animal protector in my very first dream," says Avery. "So, tell me what happened in your first dream."

"I was welcomed by a guy named Tate."

Avery abruptly interrupts, "Did you notice his incredible purple eyes? That guy's *sooo* dreamy." She giggles.

"Umm . . . no," he awkwardly replies feeling jealous that she's never said a word about his eyes. "Anyhow, as I was saying—"

"Oh . . . sorry! I cut you off. And there I go, again. Sorry!" They both laugh.

"Tate, the guy with the purple eyes," he adds, smiling, "was accompanied by another guy named Jasper."

"You got to meet Jasper. That's so cool! I haven't met the animal guardian yet. What did he look like?"

"Honestly, he looked like a trendy golf player dressed in blue."

"I think I've seen him from afar. Was he wearing a ball cap?"

"Yep!"

"Aah! That's why I couldn't see his blue hair. I'll keep an eye out for him next time I'm with animal protectors. Sorry, go on."

"They introduced themselves and transported me to different parts of the universe."

"But they didn't tell you what kind of protector you are?"

"Nope. They didn't say another word."

"That's interesting. My first experience was way different than yours. I guess they tailor awakenings to the individual. What about your other dreams?"

"In my second, I was accompanied by Zander. He was dressed in green."

She nods in agreement.

"He explained how the universe was created and how fragile our planet is. He also told me I would have to work with others to help save our planet, before it's too late."

"That's it? He didn't say anything else?"

"I think I cut that dream short. I was so freaked out that I woke up."

"I know that feeling. I've done the same thing once or twice." She smiles. "I actually saw Zander last night. He was with Willow, the human guardian, and they both explained their superpowers."

"They have superpowers?"

"Yes, and we do, too, but I don't know if I'm allowed to tell you about them. What if you haven't learned enough about the parallel dimension yet?"

"Think about it. We didn't run into each other today by happenstance. I'm sure we're supposed to learn from one another's experiences."

"You're probably right. I've been dying to tell someone anyway. I mean, I told Paige, but you know how that turned out."

"That was quite the fiasco. I'm sorry."

"Thanks. That's not important anymore, though."

"You're right. So, what's your superpower?"

"Didn't you hear through the rumour mill?"

"Honestly, I didn't pay much attention to Crissy. I figured she was making stuff up to get attention. Now that I think about it, she was quite on the nose."

They both laugh.

"So, can you actually shapeshift into a falcon?"

"Yup! When I'm in the other dimension, I can fly whenever and wherever I want."

"That's AWESOME!"

"I know! It's completely nuts!"

"What about me? What can I do?"

"As a human protector, you can't shapeshift. But when you're in the other dimension, you get to spy on people."

"What?" Pike chuckles in disbelief. "That can't be right. Can it?"

"I don't know how it works exactly, but that's what I was told last night. No one knows you're there, because you're still in the other dimension, but you get to sneak a peek on whomever you want."

"Isn't that a bit invasive?"

"That's what I thought at first, too. From what I've been told, though, you can't creep up on people in vulnerable situations. The only time you can actually have a peek is when they are okay with it."

"That's a relief! Could you imagine if I checked up on one of our teachers while they were on the toilet?"

"Pike. Yuk! Why did you put that image in my head?" Avery laughs.

"Oh, I know. Forget about our teachers." Pike laughs out loud. "You'll be the first person I check up on when I gain access to my superpowers."

"Don't you dare!" She gently nudges him, and they both laugh.

"I can't wait to have another dream. I'll have a ton of questions for whomever shows up."

"I can only imagine." Avery smiles, lowers her eyes, and tucks a few loose strands of hair behind her ear.

I'm so happy Pike decided to confide in me. Who would have guessed that one of the awoken protectors was sitting beside me in class all this time?

"Ave, are you still with me?" asks Pike, feeling his friend slip into a daydream.

"Oh, sorry," she timidly replies, feeling her cheeks blush. She breaks the tension by looking at her phone. "It's a quarter to twelve. I have to head home."

As they both pick up their bicycles, Pike summons every bit of courage he has left to ask, "Would you like to meet up tomorrow morning and talk some more?"

"I'm supposed to hang out with Jake, but I guess I can cancel."

"Really?!" Pike enthusiastically replies, trying to keep his cool. "How about we hang out in my backyard? I can text you the address."

"Sounds good. See you then." She starts to slowly pedal away.

This is incredible! I can't believe Pike's a protector like me—a guy I've known for years, who's easy to talk with, and who's actually kind of cute with those gorgeous black eyes and stylish hairdo.

CHAPTER 36

AVERY OPENS HER EYES, stretches from head to toe, and discovers that the other side of her bed is empty. She takes in a deep breath of the warm summer air that is making its way through the open windows, admiring the way the white linen curtains dance gently in the breeze, letting intermittent rays of sunlight into the bedroom. She gets up and walks to the en suite bathroom, turns on the light, and stares at the woman reflected in the mirror. Still half asleep, she ties her hair into a messy bun before making her way to the kitchen.

"Hi, honey. Are the kids still in bed?"

"Yes, they are," replies Pike. "I'm not surprised. They fell asleep past midnight."

"It was an incredible evening." She sits on her husband's lap and gently wraps her arms around his shoulders. "Thanks for organizing everything."

"Ten years is worth celebrating."

"It sure is."

Avery smiles at Pike and glances lovingly over his shoulder at the family photos. She spots Liam and Becca's handmade drawings that cover the fridge.

Over the years, Avery and Pike had stopped talking—and then stopped thinking—about their purpose, as work and family life took over. Although they have passed on their eco-friendly values to their children, they still carry the guilt of having failed to do more to protect the planet.

That afternoon, when Pike takes the kids out to shoot some hoops, Avery decides to catch up on some of the sleep she missed the night before. As she drifts off, she sees a strangely familiar light in the distance. She walks toward the light and recognizes her grandfather's house. Marcus is sitting on his porch. Avery catches her breath. It's been over twenty years since her grandfather passed away.

"Grandpa! What's going on?" Avery asks.

"Please, have a seat so we can chat," he replies, gesturing to an empty rocking chair opposite his own. "Before anything else, I'd like to tell you how proud I am of the way you are raising your beautiful children. They care so deeply about the planet."

"Thank you, Grandpa." Avery smiles, feeling happy her grandfather has been able to keep watch over her family.

"And I'm very proud of the work that Pike's company is doing to convert household garbage into fuel. It's wonderful to see him fulfilling part of his calling. But now, you must both find a way to take things to the next level."

"What do you mean? I have always tried to help the animals as much as I could, but life has got in the way. How am I supposed to find time to fulfill my purpose? I have a job, a family, and bills to pay." She tries her best to hold back her tears.

"You're being too hard on yourself. You've spent your life trying to be the best person you could be, and that's wonderful. But as an awoken protector, you must find a way to do more."

"You're right." She looks up at her grandfather's caring eyes. "I need to find a way to make a *real* difference *now*."

Avery opens her eyes to find Teagan gently shaking her awake.

"Ave, wake up! I heard you grumble from the hallway."

Feeling groggy, Avery tries to find her phone. "What time is it?"

"Almost nine."

"Shoot . . . I overslept!" She stands up. "I'm meeting Pike in half an hour!"

"I thought you were seeing Jake today?" Teagan questions, raising her eyebrows.

"It's complicated." Avery jumps out of bed and runs to the bathroom to have a lightning-quick shower.

CHAPTER 37

"MOM! I'M HEADING OUT NOW!" Avery shouts while sprinting down the stairs.

"Where are you off to?" Isabel shouts back from the living room.

"I'm going to Pike's house, remember?"

"Oh, that's right."

"I'll be back for lunch."

"Don't forget to text me when you get there, and before you head back home."

"Will do. Love you!" Avery heads out the back door, grabs her bicycle from the shed, puts on her helmet, and quickly makes her way to the main road.

I can't wait to see Pike's reaction when I tell him I dreamt we were married and had two kids. It felt so real, like we were soulmates. Pike's amazing, and he actually listens to me when I talk. He's never made me feel awkward. Not like I do when I'm with Jake. What am I thinking? I've had a crush on Jake forever. All I wanted was to be his girlfriend. But what do we have in common? Nothing, really. What am I doing? Am I actually debating breaking up with Jake?

She slows down, pulls over to the side of the road, and chucks her bike down on the grass, sitting beside it.

Everything's so easy with Pike. We have so much in common now. I don't feel like hanging out with Jake anymore. I just want to spend time with Pike.

She sighs loudly as she pulls her phone out of her pocket.

I can't believe I'm actually going to do this . . .

She texts, "*Hey, Jake. Just want to tell you that you're cool and all, but I'm going to be busy this summer. I don't have time for a boyfriend. Hugs, XO.*"

She gets up, puts her phone in her pocket, and grabs her bike. She's about to pedal away as she hears the message alert. Quickly pulling out her phone, she reads, "*No problem. I was about to text you the same thing. I've been hanging out with Paige whenever you're not around. So that's fine. I hope you enjoy your summer as much as I will.*"

Good riddance. I can't believe he was about to dump me for Paige! What a jerk!

She decides to text her little sister. "*Teag, check this out . . . I just broke up with Jake.*"

"*What? Why?*" Her sister answers.

"*Long story . . . anyhow, that's not the point. He replied that he was about to dump me for Paige. Can you believe it?*"

"*OMG! How could he? He knows how much she hurt you. Are you okay?*"

"*Yeah, whatever . . .*"

"*We need to make them pay. We should TP their houses or something ;)*"

"*LOL! It's all good. I just needed to share . . .*"

"*Let me know if you change your mind ;)*"

Avery smiles, puts her phone away, and cycles the rest of the way to Pike's house. *Teag drives me nuts sometimes, but I don't know what I'd do without her.*

Pike's sitting on his front steps, patiently awaiting her arrival. She locks her bike up and breathlessly tells him, "You'll never believe what I dreamt about last night. We were married with two kids, a boy and a girl, and you were an environmental engineer who ran a company converting garbage into fuel."

Speechless, he stares blankly, doing all he can to keep his cool and not shout, *I love you! You're perfect! Being married to you would be amazing.* Instead, he carefully replies, "That sounds like another intense dream."

"It was! It felt like a wake-up call. I know my life's purpose, and I have to start working on it. And now, I know exactly where to start."

"Really? Where?"

"Do you remember when I told you I had a feeling something weird was happening at the De La Grotta Zoo?" Pike nods in response. "Well, Skyler, one of the staff, worked at a VIP event where they served the guests food made from exotic animal meat. And we're pretty sure the animals came from the zoo."

"That's terrible!"

"Exactly! And we think they're experimenting on animals. She saw a bunch of them hooked up to machines, and they looked like they were suffering."

"That's devastating."

"I know. And once, when I shapeshifted into a falcon, I saw that they were dumping chemicals in the river."

"You know what? I overheard my mom the other day say that one of her colleagues is investigating the chemical spill. He has a feeling it's related to the zoo, but he can't prove it."

"That's exactly the problem. We can't prove anything."

"I think I can help," says Pike. "Last night, I was with Zander and Theo, the Earth guardian."

"Oh, yeah. The big muscular guy. He's really nice."

He nods in agreement. "He told me that I need to help you achieve your purpose, which will indirectly help me focus on mine. I told him we were seeing each other this morning, and he asked me to bring you with me to the parallel universe."

"I didn't know we could go together."

"Me neither, but Zander and Theo told me that we can, if we find a secluded spot where no one will see us vanish."

"But we don't disappear when we go to the other dimension. We look like we're sleeping or meditating."

"That's right. But when we travel in pairs, our bodies leave this dimension and enter the other one."

"Hmm . . . how do we get back?"

"The same way we leave."

"Okay. So where should we go?"

"Let's head to the basement. My parents won't bother us." Pike and Avery make their way into the house and head directly downstairs.

"Whoa! This is a sweet space. Where'd you get all this stuff?" She walks around the room, admiring the massive collection of action figures and movie posters, trying to avoid tripping over computer equipment and gadgets that cover the floor.

"I know. My family's a bit odd. We're all into online gaming, sci-fi movies, and superhero action figures. Sometimes, my parents, my big brother, and I end up gaming for hours until my mom finally notices the time and tells us to head to bed."

"My mom does the same thing, but at my house, we play cards and board games. She's always been worried about radiation exposure. So, we were never allowed to play with electronics. She finally let me play with a tablet when I turned eight. And even then, she would never let me play online games because of the Wi-Fi—all the games had to be pre-downloaded by her."

"Your mom would flip out if she came over here. Nothing's wired."

"My poor mom." She chuckles as she sits down on the couch next to Pike. "We often tease her that we'll have the sentence *Did you shut the Wi-Fi?* engraved on her tombstone." They both laugh, getting comfy.

"Are you ready?" Pike asks.

Avery takes a deep breath. "Ready as I'll ever be," she replies nervously.

CHAPTER 38

"SO, HOW DOES THIS WORK, exactly? Are there a series of magic words we need to say or something?" asks Avery.

"No, no." He laughs. "We need to close our eyes and hold hands, and then we need to focus on what each other's heart desires."

"But how am I supposed to know what you want?"

"I don't know exactly, but Theo said that if we open our heart and trust, it will happen," Pike says softly.

"Okay, then. Let's try this!"

He nervously puts his hands out—realizing that he's about to hold hands with his lifetime crush—and she puts hers in his. He blurts, "Your hands are *sooo* soft."

"They are?" She shrugs. "My mom's always telling me to put cream on before going to bed. I guess it works."

Feeling foolish for having said that, he quickly changes the subject. "Oops! I almost forgot." He lets go of Avery's hands and fiddles with his watch.

"What are you doing?"

"I want to set a timer to see how long we'll be *gone* for."

"Great idea! Every time I'm in the other dimension, it feels like I'm there for way longer than I actually was."

"Exactly! This way, we'll be able to know." Pike puts his hands back in hers. "Let's close our eyes, and you can count us down."

"Okay . . . three, two, one."

Nothing happens.

They wait a few more seconds . . . and still nothing.

Avery whispers. "How long is this supposed to take?"

"I don't know," he whispers back. "Try to stay in the *zone*."

A few seconds later, Avery says. "Yeah . . . this isn't working. We must be doing something wrong." She lets go of his hands and leans on the couch out of despair.

"Don't give up so easily. We can figure this out." Pike stands up and slowly starts pacing around the room. "We closed our eyes and held hands—that was the easy part. Focusing on what each other's heart desires—that's where it becomes tricky."

"Definitely! To be honest with you, I was blanking out a bit."

"Me too," he replies, sitting back down on the couch. "Okay, so what does your heart desire?"

"Gee, I don't know . . . umm . . . I saw some sick sneakers online the other day."

Pike snickers. "I think we need to think bigger than that."

"In that case, it's simple! I want to save the animals at the zoo."

"Perfect! I can easily imagine that because I feel the same way."

"Maybe that's the trick—we need to focus on a common wish."

"Okay. Let's try this again," says Pike as he puts his hands out.

"Hold on!" Avery interjects. "You need to reset your watch, first."

"Good point!" he replies, fiddling with the tiny buttons. "Okay, now I'm ready."

They hold hands and close their eyes. In unison, they focus on each other's heart's desire. Avery smiles as she feels an inexplicable connection with Pike—spinning together through space and time into another dimension. Still holding hands, they have transformed into their true selves. They open their eyes to find that they are standing on an unfamiliar planet with yellow, rocky mountains in the distance. They gaze at each other, taking in the elegant beings they have transformed into.

"You look even more amazing than I had imagined." Pike smiles.

Feeling herself blush, she responds, "Well, you look incredible."

"I do?"

"Yeah! Turn around, let me look at you. You look like a fitness model."

"It's kind of hard to tell. I've never seen my reflection." A full-length mirror magically appears. "Ha! This place never ceases to amaze me."

"You see what I mean?"

"I do look pretty cool. Don't I?" He smiles and takes a look at his outfit—a burgundy, sleeveless vest worn over a buttoned-up shirt, with a loose tie that matches his pair of slim-fit, maroon-coloured pants, worn with barefoot loafers. "Nice! Check out this faded beard and cool tapered dreads. I wonder if this is what we'll end up looking like when we grow up?"

The mirror vanishes.

"Who knows, but I'd be surprised if my hair turns that dark as I get older."

"One thing's for sure—you'll be stunning no matter your hair colour." Suddenly feeling awfully confident, Pike adds, "Do you know that you're the most beautiful girl in school?"

She giggles.

"It's true. You're very good-looking, and you always have been, and your inner being is breathtaking. I've never seen anyone look as striking as you do right now."

"Seriously?"

"Yes."

"Okay, then. Thank you." She smiles and twirls her thick, lustrous, hair.

"I can't believe I'm saying all of this. I think I'm more confident in this dimension."

"It sure sounds that way." She smiles and gently nudges him with her elbow. "And why shouldn't you be? You're an amazing guy. I'm sure girls will be fighting over you in no time."

"You think so?"

"I know so. Who wouldn't want to become the future bride of a thoughtful and handsome environmental engineer who spends his days trying to find ways to improve the planet?" They both laugh.

Feeling embarrassed, she tries to change the subject.

"Do you have any idea where we are?"

"Nope," Pike replies, trying to catch his bearings. "Cool! Look over there." He points into space. "That sun has rings. Just like Saturn."

"I don't think that's a sun," replies Avery. "I'm pretty sure that's Saturn."

"Whoa! You're right! This is unreal! That means we're on Titan."

"What's Titan?"

"It's Saturn's biggest moon."

"That's so cool!"

They look in all directions, trying to take in as much of the incredible scenery as possible. They notice a purplish-blue glow appear on their left. It's Tate and Jasper.

"Jasper! Is that really you?"

"It sure is! I'm so glad to finally meet you, Avery."

"Thanks for coming, you two," interjects Tate. "We have lots to show you, so I'm going to get straight to the point."

"We need to save the animals at the De La Grotta Zoo, don't we?" Avery queries.

"That's right," replies Jasper. "We need your help, and we need it now. Sadly, you've only uncovered the tip of the iceberg."

CHAPTER 39

"THE NEW OWNERS have been illegally trading endangered animals for decades," states Jasper. "And three years ago, they started to acquire zoological parks across the world. They figured that hiding behind family-friendly wildlife parks would help them easily move animals around the globe without attracting attention, and they were right."

"The zoo where you volunteer is their most recent purchase, bringing the total number to six," jumps in Tate. "They also have a presence in the US, Brazil, Spain, Kenya, and Australia."

"We've been keeping an eye on the owners for years," adds Jasper. "But we've never been able to prove what they've been doing. Which is where you two come in."

"I don't think I'm following," Avery interjects. "You're not expecting us to gather evidence. Are you?"

"That's exactly what we need you to do," replies Tate.

"But how?" asks Pike. "We're only fifteen years old."

"That's exactly why it's going to work. No one will suspect you. To boot, you know the zoo inside and out, and Pike's mother is a detective. So, if you bring her solid evidence, there's a good chance she'll take you seriously."

Jasper waves his hands, and an image appears in the air in front of them.

"Whoa! That came out of nowhere. What kind of tech is this?" Pike tries to touch the translucent screen. He inspects behind it, trying to figure out how it's made.

"Pike, come on," Avery teases. "This isn't technology. We're in another dimension where we can shapeshift and see our past lives. I think we're way beyond tech."

"Ha! You're right. I'm still getting used to this place." He laughs.

"Before we begin," Tate says seriously, "I want to warn you. Some of what you're about to see may be disturbing, especially for an animal protector."

Avery swallows hard, not wanting to see anything distressing, but knowing that they need her to be brave. "I'm assuming you wouldn't show me if you didn't have to."

"That's true. Thank you for understanding." Tate appreciates her courage.

"Okay, I'm ready."

"Each zoo has a uniquely designed hunting arena. For example, one has a desert theme, another looks like the Arctic, and one location even has an aquarium that simulates the ocean, where customers choose which shark they will hunt and kill."

Dumbfounded, Pike asks, "How can there be so many people that think this is acceptable?"

"That's one thing we still don't understand," Jasper replies.

"I think I know! They tricked my friend Skyler into signing a nondisclosure agreement. If she breaks it, they will sue her."

"Can they do that?" asks Pike.

"I don't know, but she's really freaked out."

"That explains it," says Jasper. "These poor people must feel trapped."

"Skyler does, for sure. They also told her that if she quits before the end of her contract, she'll have to give back the money they paid her, plus a penalty of ten thousand dollars. So, there's no way she can quit."

"These people are awful. They don't care about anyone or anything," says Pike.

"There's more for us to show you," adds Tate, as dozens of images appear. "The company produces illegal animal byproducts. The zoo located in Brazil, the one in Kenya, and the one in Australia farm animals to create exotic fur products."

"But why? No one wears fur anymore," says Pike. "That went out of style years ago when people realized how cruel it was."

"Not exactly," interjects Jasper. "You're right, very few people actually wear fur these days, but there's still a big market for products such as wall hangings, carpets, and bedding made of fur. Basically, the market has gone from clothes to interior decor."

Speechless, Avery shakes her head in disbelief.

"The zoo located in the US, the one in Spain, and the De La Grotta Zoo specialize in creating bizarre crossbreeds. This is so unnatural—most of the animals they breed die within a few weeks. They use these failures in the exotic meat market."

"That's enough. I can't hear any more." Avery cries out, leaning into Pike, who wraps his arms around her. "Don't they know that animals are intelligent creatures who understand what happens around them? That they fear for their lives and suffer when they are helpless to save the ones they love? This is too much for me to handle. Can you please stop?"

"I know how much you hate seeing the evil side of humans, but please bear with us for a few more minutes. We're almost done."

Avery slowly looks up from Pike's comforting embrace and nods. "Okay . . . if I have to."

"Don't worry, Ave. I've got you. We'll get through this together. Jasper and Tate are right. We need to know what those evil people are doing so we can gather all the evidence needed to put them in jail."

She exhales deeply. "Okay, you're right. I can do this. I'm ready to hear the rest."

"I'm proud of you, Avery," says Tate, and the images change. "Each zoo has a Body Enhancement and Rejuvenation Centre, where wealthy people pay to receive animal-based treatments that promise to make them look and feel younger. Some of the procedures include shark-spleen-oil injections that are used to eliminate wrinkles—they get three treatments out of every shark they kill. They perform gorilla-muscle implants that double the size of muscles without having to do any exercise—they get up to five transplants out of every gorilla they kill."

"They also offer sloth-nail bed replacements," jumps in Jasper. "This procedure surgically replaces human nail beds with the ones from sloths, creating impeccable 'natural' nails ready for any type of manicure—they get one treatment out of every sloth they kill. There are also monkey-hair transplants. This is by far the most popular treatment for men. They remove hair follicles from monkeys and transplant them onto human scalps—they get two transplants out of every monkey they kill."

"That's enough. We get it," Pike says firmly, gently squeezing Avery's hand. "How can these people live with themselves, knowing that animals have been killed so they can feel better about the way they look?" Pike shakes his head.

"They're lost. They think that if they look better, they'll feel better," replies Tate. "By putting a stop to this, you'll be saving countless animals, and you'll also be serving humanity by preventing these people from using animals for 'quick fixes' to try and overcome their feelings of inadequacy."

"It's a lot of responsibility." Avery sighs.

"We believe in you." Jasper smiles reassuringly.

"I guess there's no time to lose," says Pike. He looks at Avery, and they join hands, focusing on each other's heart's desire.

CHAPTER 40

PIKE AND AVERY reappear in the basement.

"Are you okay? That was a lot to take in."

The kindness in his voice is too much, and Avery's eyes flood with tears. "That was horrible. How can these people sleep at night? I don't understand how anyone can be so cruel."

Trying to lighten the mood, he says, "Check it out! We were only gone for thirty-five seconds."

She smirks, still crying. Pike puts his arm around her and rocks her gently. "That was rough. I can only imagine how difficult it must have been for you."

Avery swallows hard and steels herself. "Now that I know how evil those people are, nothing will stop me from completing this mission."

Pike squeezes her extra tight, proud of how strong she is. "So, where do we start?" he asks.

"I don't know exactly, but one thing's for sure, we can't do this alone."

"What about your friend, Skyler?"

"Definitely. We can't tell her about the other dimension, but I know how desperate she is to do something. So, I don't think she'll ask too many questions. She'll be relieved there's something she can do to help save the animals."

"Do you think we could meet up with her tomorrow morning and figure out a plan?"

"I'll text her now and see if she's free." Avery grabs her phone and messages Skyler. As she looks at her phone, she sees that it's eleven-thirty. "Oh, goodness! Where did the time go! I promised my mom I'd be back by lunch. I have to run!"

"Before you leave, I want to tell you that I'm really happy we're working on this together."

"Me too. I wish the animals weren't suffering, but at least we can do something to help."

"And hopefully, we won't wake up one day and realize we wasted half our life not doing enough," he adds, trying his best to make her smile.

"That's true," she gives him a half smile in return.

Pike follows Avery out the front door and watches as she unlocks her bicycle.

"Oh, by the way, I broke up with Jake this morning on the way over to your house."

"You're kidding? What happened?"

"I realized that I don't have much in common with him, and I'd prefer spending my summer with you. I hope that wasn't too forward of me?"

Trying to keep his cool, Pike replies, "No, of course not. I think we'll be pretty busy with all this saving the world stuff."

"I think you're right." Avery tilts her head to the side, smiles, and cycles away.

"Man," he whispers to himself as he turns to head inside. "I can't believe Ave broke up with Jake to spend time with me. With me . . . is this really happening?!"

CHAPTER 41

THE NEXT MORNING, Pike and Skyler meet up at Avery's house. They head to the backyard so they can chat in private.

Pike and Skyler introduce themselves. A few minutes later, Avery asks. "Anything new at the zoo?"

"Sadly, yes. I was asked to clean one of the operating rooms yesterday. There was a walk-in freezer filled with frozen fetuses, but I didn't recognize any of the animals. It was so strange. They looked like a mix of rabbits and penguins."

"They sound like some of the perverted crossbreeds we've heard about." Pike nods.

"Where did you hear that?" Skyler looks puzzled.

"Oh . . . from my mom. She's a police detective. They've been keeping an eye on the zoo ever since we had that chemical spill."

"Oh, my goodness. This is even worse than I thought." Skyler sighs.

"Have you noticed anything else out of the ordinary?" asks Pike.

"No, but I've been offered an overnight shift for the upcoming VIP event."

"Oh, no!" interjects Avery. "That's when guests will be hunting the animals in the arena. We have to stop them. Pike, do you think we have enough to convince your mom to arrest them?"

"No, we don't. We need to get proof."

"How are we supposed to do that?" asks Avery.

"We need to take as many pictures as possible of everything they're up to."

"No one's allowed to take their phones into the restricted area. They have scanners. There's no way I can take pictures or videos." Skyler looks crestfallen.

"That's not a problem. My dad has a ton of miniature cameras that we could easily hide and won't trigger any of the sensors."

"And . . . why would your dad have these?" Skyler is skeptical.

"He's a robotic engineer. He builds and tests advanced technologies, and he's always bringing home surplus equipment and prototypes to work on. We even built a drone together a few months ago."

"Your dad sounds really cool," Skyler states.

"He is."

"Won't he notice that some of his stuff is missing?" asks Avery.

"I don't think so. If we pick from some of the older boxes, I'm sure he'll never know. Besides, it's not like we're stealing anything. We'll bring everything back in a few days."

"Could we put one of those cameras on your drone?"

"That's a great idea. And if we use an infrared camera, we could fly it at night and see what happens when the zoo's closed. We could also set up concealed cameras around the zoo that will send a live feed to a computer."

"It sounds like we have all the tech we need. Now what?" asks Avery.

"We need to get everything set up as soon as possible. The VIP event is coming up in less than three weeks," Skyler replies.

"In that case we need to get this done by the end of this week. Otherwise, my mom won't have time to investigate and arrest everyone before the event."

"Okay then," says Skyler. "There's no time to waste."

"et's head over to my house right now and work out exactly what we need. That way, I can make sure everything is tested and fully charged by the morning."

"Nice. I'll have time to come by your house to pick up the equipment before my shift. The summer schedule starts tomorrow, and I'll be working from noon to eight."

"And I'll be volunteering every Wednesday, Friday, and Sunday from noon to five."

"That's perfect. We can install the video cameras tomorrow and capture as much evidence as possible over the next few days, then take them down before leaving the zoo on Friday evening," says Skyler. "If you want, I could pick you both up tomorrow around eleven-thirty."

"That works for me," replies Avery.

"Hold on," Pike interjects. "I think we're trying to do too much. We'll need some help."

"To do what?" asks Skyler.

"Someone will need to monitor the live video feeds from the concealed cameras. I'll need to fly my drone to capture footage. And someone will need to download and edit the pictures you take in the restricted areas. And once all of this is done, we'll need to—"

"Hold on," interrupts Avery. Immediately followed by, "Teag! Where do you think you're going?"

"I'm bored. I want to hang with you guys," Teagan says, exiting the house and making her way to the group. "I'm Teagan. You can call me *Teag*, for short—"

"Seriously! Can't you see we're trying to have a private conversation?"

"It's okay, Ave," adds Skyler. "Let her stay for a few minutes."

"Thank you!" says Teagan, smirking at her big sister and grabbing a seat. "So . . . what are your names? No, wait! Let me guess."

"You're Skyler. Ave's boss. Right?"

"You can call me Sky. I'm not Avery's boss. I'm her volunteer mentor."

"Same thing," Teagan teasingly dismisses. "And you are?"

"I'm Pike. Ave and I are—"

"No way! You're the infamous Pike who's had a crush on Ave since *forever*!"

"Teag! Shut up!!" squawks Avery.

"Isn't that interesting," jumps in Skyler, elbowing Pike as he tries to hide his mortification.

Not realizing that she's caused an extremely uncomfortable situation for two of the three, Teagan asks, "So, what are you guys talking about?"

"Nothing. Go away!" states Avery.

"Wait," interjects Skyler, "maybe she can help us."

"For sure! What can I do?" Teagen eagerly interjects.

"No way," adds Avery. "It's way too dangerous. She's barely thirteen."

"Hey! I can do a lot more than you give me credit for, sis. I'm at the top of my class, you know!"

"This is nothing like schoolwork."

"Actually, it's not that far off," jumps in Pike who's finally managed to put his embarrassment aside to focus on the mission. "Maybe she could help us package all the evidence in a way that's useful for my mom."

"We're capturing evidence?" Teagan asks enthusiastically.

"No. *We* are," replies Avery. "You're not even officially part of the team yet. Go sit on the deck for a minute so we can chat."

Teagan doesn't miss a beat. She runs to the steps, sits, and waits impatiently.

"So, what are we thinking?" asks Pike.

"I like her! I say she's in!" says Skyler.

"To be honest," replies Avery, "she can be a total pain in the butt, and she obviously has no filter for her big mouth, but she's really mature for her age. And trust me, when we tell her what's going on at the zoo, she'll do anything she can to help us stop them."

"Perfect," says Skyler, waving at their new teammate.

"Yay!" states Teagan, quickly making her way back to the group. "So, what's happening at the zoo?"

"You heard us?" asks Avery.

"Of course, I did. You know I have *bionic* ears. And besides, our yard is tiny."

The group laughs—Avery shakes her head and rolls her eyes.

"So, when do we start?" Teagan eagerly asks.

"Right now!" answers Pike. "Let's head over to my house."

CHAPTER 42

GUNG-HO FOR THE DAY'S EVENTS, Teagan's been staring out the window for the past fifteen minutes.

"They're here! Let's go, Ave!" shouts Teagan as she sprints out the door.

"I'm coming. Hold your horses," replies Avery, grabbing her things. She hollers, "Mom! Eric! We're leaving!"

The door slams behind her, before they can answer.

"Morning, girls!" says Skyler, resting her arm on the open window of her car. Pike lowers the front seat and climbs into the back.

"Pike, why did you change seats?" asks Avery.

"I wanted to leave the front passenger seat for one of you."

"Shotgun!" shouts Teagan.

Avery shakes her head at her sister, smiles at Pike, and says, "Aren't you sweet?"

A moment later, Skyler asks, "Is everyone buckled up?"

The group simultaneously answers, "Yup!"

As the car pulls away, Teagan exclaims, "Thank you so much for including me, guys. Yesterday was really cool. I still can't believe you have access to all that tech, Pike."

"You can come over to my house anytime and tinker with the gadgets. My dad loves teaching people about electronics."

"Seriously? I would love that!"

"That's really nice of you," whispers Avery.

"So, how's everyone feeling this morning?" asks Skyler.

"I'm a bit nervous," replies Pike. "I hardly slept. I couldn't stop going over everything we're supposed to do today. I'm worried we might get caught."

"Me too," says Avery.

"Me three, but I think we have a solid plan," adds Skyler.

Avery gives Pike her hat. "Check it out. Here's where I put the camera."

"Well done! I can barely see it."

"Thanks. I'm happy with the way it turned out."

"And look inside," adds Avery. "I tucked the back end of the camera in the headband. So, I can pretend to scratch the side of my head whenever I want to take a picture, and no one will know."

"That's clever!" replies Pike. "And what about you, Sky? Do you feel comfortable with your camera pen?"

"Yes, I practised last night. Whenever I want to take a picture and someone's around, I'll cross my arms and point the pen in the direction I want to shoot."

"This is so exciting!" exclaims Teagan. They enter the De La Grotta Zoo's parking lot.

As Avery and Skyler carry out their duties, Pike and Teagan install the hidden cameras in various spots around the zoo. As previously arranged, they meet up by the reptile house around two-thirty—halfway through Avery's shift.

"Hey, guys. How's it going?" Avery asks Pike and Teagan as she sees them approach.

"Great. Everything's up and running." Teagan smiles. "How's it going for you two?"

"Nothing incriminating yet," replies Skyler, "but I'm working in the restricted area later this afternoon, once Avery's volunteer shift is over."

"Right, well I guess we'd better go before we get behind with our work," says Avery. "We don't want to raise any suspicions."

"You're right. We'll see you at the front gate around five," Pike replies.

CHAPTER 43

THE NEXT MORNING, the group meets up by video chat before Skyler starts her shift at the zoo.

"The good news is that the four video feeds work well. There's nothing incriminating so far, but maybe we'll get lucky today. The bad news is, only a handful of the pictures you took came out," Pike says sadly.

"No! You can't be serious. Did the pics of the vet clinic turn out?" Skyler asks, tearing up.

He silently shakes his head.

"Shoot! What about the ones of the disgusting meat packages?"

"Actually, those are the only ones that turned out okay."

"What happened?" asks Avery.

"My guess is that there wasn't enough lighting in the other rooms, because a lot of them are blurred."

"I can't believe it." Skyler tears up. "It wasn't easy to get all those pictures. I don't know if I can do it again."

"It's okay, Sky. It's not your fault. You did your best."

"Thanks, Teag. You're sweet."

"What about the ones I took?" asks Avery.

"Sorry, Ave, but none of the pictures you took can help build a case."

"That's what I figured. Nothing happened in the main zoo area."

"All the illegal stuff takes place in the restricted area," Skyler cries out. "That's why they never get caught. I'm sorry, guys, but I think we're in over our heads. Maybe we should stop."

"No! We can do this," states Pike. "We still have two days left. These cameras are finicky. You just need to make sure there's plenty of light when you take pictures today, the same type of lighting you had in the meat locker."

"Okay. I'll try," replies Skyler, sighing heavily, and feeling lucky to be surrounded by her very own cheering squad. "Oh...Ave, I can't believe I almost forgot to tell you. I saw Kiki and Koko yesterday after your shift ended."

"You did?"

"Who are we talking about?" asks Teagan.

"You know . . . the baby koalas I showed you on my phone."

"Oh, yeah . . . they're so cute. Are they okay?"

"They looked way better than the other poor animals stuck in the restricted area, but they looked scared, and I could hear them cry through the door."

"Ah, man!!! Those poor babies! That breaks my heart!" Avery's eyes glisten with tears.

"Don't worry. I'll get better pictures today. We'll be able to stop them soon. Keep your fingers crossed for me."

"We sure will," replies Teagan.

"You've got this, Sky!" Pike reassures her, smiling.

"I'd better head to work. If I get there a bit early, then I can get some of my tasks out of the way and concentrate on getting these photos," Skyler says, determination in her eyes.

"That's the spirit," says Avery. "While you're doing that, we'll head over to Pike's and watch the live feed from the hidden video cameras. Hopefully we'll have more luck with that footage today."

CHAPTER 44

LATER THAT DAY, Skyler manages to sneak out during her break to make a call.

"Hey, guys. Sky's calling," Avery says, relieved by the welcome distraction from watching endless hours of the zoo video feed.

"Put her on speaker," says Pike.

"Hey," Skyler whispers, "you won't believe what happened. I've managed to get a sample of the chemicals in the tanker. I almost got caught, but I hid in the janitor's closet. While I was in there, I overheard them saying that the chemical tank will be emptied tonight."

"I knew you could do it," Teagan gushes.

"Thank you," Skyler replies happily.

"The timing's perfect. I'm flying the drone tonight. I'm hoping to get some interesting footage before the sun sets. After that, I'll switch to the infrared camera."

"That's great," says Avery. "Sky, were you able to get some more pictures?"

"Not yet, but I still have three hours left of my shift."

"We're keeping our fingers crossed for you," says Teagan.

"What about you? Did you guys see anything on the live video feeds?"

"Nothing so far, but we'll keep watching," Pike reassures her.

"Perfect. I have to head back. See you all tomorrow."

Later that night, Avery sits on her bed, feeling nervous. She checks the time again, and then prepares herself to meditate. As soon as she feels herself pull into the alternate dimension, she shapeshifts and perches herself on top of the monkey zone. She looks in every direction and notices Pike's drone approaching. She takes flight over the zoo and makes her way to the river, guiding Pike along the way.

Everything goes perfectly. She flies silently ahead of Pike's drone, making sure the coast is clear so he can capture the video footage of the tanker dumping the chemicals in the river. He even manages to zoom in on the driver's face.

As she slips back into her body and her bed, Avery quickly sinks into a deep sleep. It's been a long day—but a rewarding one. They are finally starting to put the pieces of the puzzle together.

CHAPTER 45

THE NEXT MORNING, the sisters arrive bright and early at Pike's house. They stopped in at Skyler's house on the way to pick up the film from her hidden camera.

"Do you mind if I'm the one who scans Sky's pictures? I'm pretty sure I remember the steps you showed me yesterday," Teagan asks enthusiastically.

"Sure thing, Teag! Ave, do you mind keeping an eye on the live feeds so I can work on the drone video?"

"Of course! Whatever helps," Avery replies, settling down on a beanbag in front of the screens that Pike has set up.

After an hour of staring at the video feeds, Avery calls out to her sister, "Hey, Teag, how are you getting on with Sky's pictures?"

"Really good. She got a bunch of great pics this time. I've just finished putting a selection of the most incriminating ones together. I'll show you in a few minutes."

"Nice! And what about you, Pike? How's the drone footage?"

"Some sections are a bit dark, but I'm working my magic. We've definitely got some good evidence."

"What a relief." Avery turns her attention back to the live feeds. "Guys! Where's the volume on this thing? Can we zoom in?"

"What's going on?"

"Hurry, Pike! It's Mr. Fleming and Mr. Perdue. Are we sure this is recording?"

Pike quickly takes control of the mouse and confirms that the feed from the camera by the monkey enclosure is being recorded.

"Can you zoom in any closer?"

"Good point, Teag. We have to clearly see their faces."

"That's perfect," says Avery, as Pike closes in on the two men.

Pike turns the volume up, just in time to hear Mr. Fleming say, "Seriously?"

"I know," responds Mr. Perdue. "The driver was picked up trying to cross the border. So, we've lost all of those monkeys, and the rest of the crew are really nervous. They're worried that the driver's flipped on them, and that the police will be watching every move they make. So, we're back to square one."

"We have four hair transplants scheduled for next week. Do you know how much money those procedures bring in? It's not rocket science, Perdue. Just ship a few monkeys from one of our other zoos," states Mr. Fleming, shaking his head and rolling his eyes.

"Yes, sir," Mr. Perdue replies. "I'll get a hold of Brazil right away."

"This is perfect," Pike says.

"*Shhhh.* They're still talking," Teagan says, anxious not to miss a word.

"Do you have an update on the auction?"

"We have received several bids in the last two days."

"I knew there would be interest for that odd couple."

"The latest bid is for twenty-five thousand dollars, but there's a catch. The bidder is requesting that we mount the two babies in their mother's arms."

"The auction listing clearly states that the lot is for a set of rare, white, twin koalas, stuffed and mounted in a tree. The mother is a separate lot."

Dumbfounded, Avery repeatedly shakes her head and exhales the words, "No, no, no, no, no!"

"If they want to include the mother in the display, then they'll need to bid separately for her."

"Understood, Mr. Fleming. I will reply to the bidder and advise them that they will need to place an additional bid for the mother."

"These people are horrible," exclaims Avery. "I can't take it anymore. I can't."

"They've given us more than enough, Avery. They've said each other's names, and they've spoken openly about what they're doing," Pike consoles her, as he gently puts his hands on her shoulders.

"He's right. We've got them," Teagan nods.

"I hope so." Avery sighs. "I can't take much more of this—" Her words are interrupted by the doorbell. She looks at the time. "It's eleven-thirty. That must be Skyler. She said she'd pick me up so we can head to the zoo together." She quickly makes her way to the staircase, followed by Pike and Teagan.

Pike opens the front door. "Sky!" exclaims Teagan. "You won't believe it. We caught Mr. Fleming and Mr. Perdue on camera."

"For real?"

"Yup! And the pics you took yesterday are perfect, and so is Pike's drone footage."

"Sweet! Do we have enough evidence now?"

"We have a lot," answers Pike.

"Okay, so we're sticking with the plan. Ave and I will capture as much evidence as we can during this shift, and then we're pulling the cameras."

"That's right," adds Pike. "Be safe, you two!"

Avery and Skyler make their way to the car. As soon as Skyler backs out of Pike's driveway, Avery bursts into tears.

"What's wrong, Ave? It sounds as though we have the evidence we need. We're going to get these guys arrested. Aren't you happy?" Skyler consoles her.

"I'll believe it when I see it. We're doing all of this, but we don't know if it'll be enough."

"I know. I feel the same way. But at least we're trying."

"I guess." Avery sobs. "It's unreal. These people are even worse than we thought. I don't know what I'll do if I run into Mr. Fleming today. You won't believe what he's planning on doing with Kiki and Koko."

CHAPTER 46

PIKE AND TEAGAN have their hands full sorting through the rest of the footage and collating the information to present it to Pike's mother.

Pike clicks through the presentation. "Great work, Teag! It looks awesome. This should make it easy for my mom to see if there's enough to work with."

As they are coming to the end of the presentation, Teagan notices some movement on one of the hidden cameras.

"What's going on over there?" she asks as the live feed cuts out.

"It looks like someone found one of the cameras."

"Oh, no! We need to warn them," Teagan says, urgently texting the group chat.

"No! You can't. Now that they've found one of the cameras, they're going to be on alert. What if they decide to check all the employees' phones? They'll see that you tried to warn them."

"Okay. Let's try calling instead."

Teagan calls her sister, listening impatiently until it rings out. "She isn't picking up."

"Same here. Sky's phone is going straight to voicemail."

"Oh, no! Look," says Pike. The feed from another camera drops out, followed a few minutes later by the third, and then the fourth.

"This is freaking me out," Teagan wails. "We need to do something!"

"We can't. But it's almost five. Avery's shift will be over in a few minutes. Let's wait another fifteen minutes or so. If we haven't heard from them by then, we'll head down to the zoo to meet her."

"Okay." Teagan is hesitant, scared.

A few minutes later, Teagan's phone rings.

She immediately answers and blurts out, "What's going on? Are you okay? Where are you? We've been worried sick!"

"Whoa! What's going on?" Avery asks anxiously.

"Are you guys okay?"

"Yeah, we're fine. Sky said she had a headache so she could finish at the same time as me. We'll be pulling up to Pike's house in two minutes."

"Hey, guys," says Avery, stepping out of Skyler's car, smiling ear to ear. "You're not going to believe the crazy shift we just had."

"Hold on!" Teagan cuts in. "You can't just start talking about your day like nothing happened! We were really worried about you."

"Oh, Teag. I'm so sorry," Avery says sympathetically, realizing how worried her little sister had been. She reaches over and grabs her sister's hand. "You've seen a lot of freaky things these past few days. Are you okay?"

"It's hard, you know? I spent the afternoon looking at disgusting pictures." Teagan wipes her nose and sniffs a few times.

"I'm extremely proud of you three," Skyler says. "I don't think I would have been able to do this when I was thirteen or fifteen."

"We didn't really have a choice." Teagan sniffles.

"Of course, you did."

"Not really. We had to stop these horrible monsters."

"A lot of people say they want to make the world a better place, but they never do anything about it. Believe me, you guys are the real deal."

"Thanks for saying that." Teagan shrugs, half-smiles, and tries to stop crying. "Okay, tell us about your shift."

"There were a bunch of employees missing today," explains Avery. "I had to clean out the enclosures on my own, because Sky was the only volunteer mentor, and she needed to help out the vet team with an upcoming operation."

"So, I started my shift in the restricted area along with Hazel and another assistant. At one point, they were called away to attend an emergency in the elephant enclosure."

"But it was a fake emergency," jumps in Avery. "I called it in."

"You did?" states Teagan.

"No way!" adds Pike. "What did you say?"

"One of the elephants is due to go into labour, so I called the vet clinic and told them that the pregnant elephant looked like she might be ready to give birth."

"I love it!" Pike laughs.

"It was perfect," jumps in Skyler. "I told Hazel I was happy to keep prepping the operating room while she and the other assistant went to check on the elephant. Which meant that I was alone in the clinic."

"Did you plan this whole thing ahead of time?" asks Teagan.

"Yes. Once we found out that Sky was going to spend part of her shift in the restricted area, we quickly sketched out a plan," replies Avery, feeling very proud.

"And it worked out even better than we'd hoped. My goal was to take more pictures of the animals, but I hit the jackpot. Hazel was in such a rush to get to the elephant enclosure that she didn't log out of her computer."

"And?" Teagan asks, breathless with anticipation.

"I accessed the client database."

"SERIOUSLY?!" Pike yells, excited. "You hit the mother lode!"

"Yes! I got part of the client tracking sheets, some signed confidentiality agreements, and a few pictures of clients with the animals they'd killed."

"That's incredible!"

"I know. I could hardly believe it!"

"But what about the hidden cameras?" asks Teagan, whose patience is quickly running out. "We still don't know what happened."

"Oh, yes, so check this out! At about four-thirty, Sky and I were getting ready to take the cameras down before our shift ended. Then, we heard one of the security guards say over the radio that he had found a hidden camera."

"Oh, no!" says Teagan.

"Yeah! I was really freaked out."

"We both were!" Skyler jumps in.

"We managed to get the rest of the cameras without being noticed," continues Avery.

"So, they only found one?" inquires Teagan.

"Yup!"

"Then what?"

"We made our way to the front gate, because our shifts had ended."

"That's a relief!" Teagan sighed.

"Yes, but then, two security guards stopped us just as we got to the gate."

"Oh, no!"

"Yeah, but they just had a quick look in our bags and let us pass."

"I swear, it's as though someone was looking over us," says Skyler, in disbelief. Avery and Pike lock eye contact and smile.

"Man . . . that was close," says Teagan.

"Yeah, too close! My mom would have grounded me for life if either of you got into trouble trying to gather evidence."

CHAPTER 47

THE NEXT MORNING, Pike anxiously wakes up early. Trying to set the stage for his upcoming conversation with his mother, Lylyan, Pike decided to make breakfast.

"Hi, Mom," Pike says cheerfully when his mother walks in, bleary eyed, clumsily tying the belt of her dressing gown. "I made pancakes, and they're keeping warm in the oven."

"You did?" Lylyan opens the oven door and takes in the sweet smell. "Isn't that nice?" She leans in and gives her son a kiss on the forehead. "What's the special occasion?"

"It's not exactly a special occasion, but there's something I need to share with you, and I hope you're not going to be mad."

"Hmm . . . I should have guessed you were up to something. Pancakes for no reason was too good to be true."

Trying to lighten the mood, Pike says cheekily, "I was planning on making pancakes anyway."

"Of course, you were." She laughs.

"Okay, seriously, Mom. I need to talk to you, and I really need you to listen without interrupting. Okay?"

She takes a deep breath and says, "Before you start, I can see this isn't easy for you. So, I want to thank you for being courageous and for telling me, even though you think I might get upset."

Pike nods.

"Try to relax," adds Lylyan. "I'll do my best not to interrupt you. I promise."

He breathes deeply. "You know that I've been hanging out a lot with Avery?"

Lylyan nods.

"Okay. Well, you know how Avery is a volunteer at the De La Grotta Zoo?"

She nods again, conscious that she promised not to interrupt.

"So, Avery and Skyler, another girl who works at the zoo, noticed a bunch of weird stuff happening over there after the new owners took over. But it was really hard to prove what they were doing. So, we decided to gather evidence that you can use to throw these people in jail."

Trying to respect her son's wishes, Pike's mother raises her hand, like a schoolgirl waiting to be called on by her teacher.

"Hold on, Mom. I'm not done."

Using every bit of self-control she has, she bites her lower lip and inhales deeply, just as her husband walks into the kitchen.

"Andrew, your timing's perfect. Please have a seat. Pike's about to tell us something I think we both need to hear."

"Okay," replies Pike's father, pulling up a chair next to his wife.

"So, like I was saying. There's animal cruelty happening at the zoo, and I have proof."

"What?" interjects Andrew. "What's he talking about?"

"Hold on, honey. Pike has asked that we wait until he's finished explaining before we ask any questions."

"Thanks, Mom. You know how you had a feeling the zoo had something to do with the chemical dump in the river a few months ago?

Well, you were right. I have video footage that I shot with the drone Dad and I built."

"You were in on this, and you didn't tell me!" Lylyan turns to Pike's father.

Andrew replies, "Hold on, honey. I had no idea. I helped him build the drone, but I didn't know anything about filming criminal activity."

"It's true. Dad didn't know anything about what we've been doing. I didn't want to worry either of you until we had enough proof. And look, it's all here." Pike flips open his laptop.

"Hold on a minute. I'm really disappointed. You could have gotten into real trouble."

"Mom, I knew you would react that way. That's why I asked you to please not say anything until I'm done."

She shakes her head in disbelief.

"It's okay, Lylyan. Let's hear him out. It's too late now anyway."

She sighs heavily. "Okay, fine. Go on. We're listening."

"We have almost one hundred hours of raw video saved on this laptop, which I edited down to about fifteen minutes to highlight the most incriminating evidence."

"Incriminating evidence! You sound like a detective," Andrew says teasingly. "I think you've been watching too many cop shows."

"Dad, come on! This is serious." Pike continues, opening the other laptop, "And here, you'll see the pictures Skyler took in the zoo's restricted area. This is where the gross stuff happens. They don't allow smartphones down there. So, I borrowed a few of dad's spy cameras."

"You did?"

"Don't worry. I only took the old equipment you never use, and I put it back last night."

"I'm not upset about that. I just can't believe it."

"Pike, did you stop to think for a second how dangerous this was?" asks Lylyan. "Why didn't you tell us what you were doing?"

"Because you would have tried to stop us," Pike replies truthfully.

"He's got a point, Lylyan."

She sighs. Speechless.

Trying to lighten the mood, Pike adds, "Anyhow, what's done is done." He smiles and continues, "I think you can build a pretty strong case against them, with all the evidence we've managed to pull together."

"Okay. Fine. Leave everything with me," states Lylyan. "Putting a stop to what's happening at the De La Grotta Zoo takes priority. But don't think you're getting off that easily. We're going to have a serious conversation about a suitable punishment for you."

CHAPTER 48

LATER THAT MORNING, Avery, Teagan, Skyler, and Pike sit squashed up together on the bench along one side of Pike's kitchen table, with his parents facing them.

Pike's mother clears her throat. "First off, I want to say that what you did was extremely dangerous. You could have gotten caught, and things could have gone extremely badly. Skyler, you're much older than the others. You really should have known better."

"You're right, Detective Williams. But we couldn't just stand by and do nothing. I know it was risky, but I hope we've given you enough to stop these guys."

"The drone footage may be enough to get a warrant to take samples from the tankers, but unfortunately, I don't think we can go any further than that."

"But what about the chemical sample I took?"

"What chemical sample?" responds Lylyan.

"Oh! It's in the basement. I'll be right back." Pike quickly runs downstairs.

"I was able to grab a bit of the chemical as it was being poured into the tanker, just a few hours before the truck headed for the river. I don't know what it is, but it smells like a mix of hair bleach and pickled beets."

Pike runs into the kitchen with a small, glass container filled with bright-yellow, viscous liquid. "Can you have this tested at the precinct?"

"Yes, I sure can," replies Lylyan, who is trying her best not to show how impressed she is by this resourceful group.

"This is amazing," proudly interjects Andrew. "You guys did awesome!"

"Hold on. This is far from over. There's no way to prove that the liquid came from the zoo or that it was dumped into the river. That said, I think it could help Detective Taylor move along with his investigation."

"Really?" interjects Skyler.

"Let's hope so. He may be able to link this liquid with the residue his team found on the riverbank. His current theory is that whoever is dumping these chemicals adjusted the composites after part of the city had to be evacuated a few months ago."

"I don't get it," says Teagan.

"In other words," replies Andrew, "if they dilute the yellow goo so it smells less and it isn't as harmful to animals, no one will notice, and it won't cause another evacuation."

"*Aaahhh!*"

"And they're probably dumping less at once and going deeper with their hose," adds Andrew. "This way, the chemical follows the river's natural current, and is spread across a greater surface."

"That's pretty much what Detective Taylor's scientific consultant told him last week. She also said that the culprits are probably dumping in different areas on the water bank. So, it makes it harder for us to trace dead animals and waterbirds that show up on several kilometres of shore, compared to when we found all the carcasses in one location."

"Great! So, they're getting smarter," sarcastically interjects Pike.

Desperately seeking more information, Avery asks, "And what about all the pictures Sky took at the zoo? Can you use any of those?"

"Unfortunately, everything you captured in the zoo's restricted area is horrendous, but none of it is illegal."

"How can killing endangered animals be legal?" Skyler says angrily.

"Hold on. Are you saying that some of the animals in the pictures are on the protected species list?"

"Yes. The previous owners took the mandate of caring for threatened species very seriously. At least four of the animals in the photos are on the list."

"That's good to know, but we'd still need to prove that the zoo's owners are responsible for these deaths, otherwise—"

"Sky!" interrupts Teagan. "Tell her about the stuff you downloaded from Hazel's computer."

"Good idea. Pike, did you show your mom the pictures of the hunting arena?"

"There's a hunting arena?" Andrew looks horrified.

"Yes, and there's one in every zoo they own," replies Avery. "It's completely disgusting. Clients get to choose which animal they kill."

"Twice a year, each zoo hosts a VIP event where clients are invited to hunt and kill their prey, before attending an exotic meat tasting where the dishes are prepared using the animals that have been killed," says Skyler. "The next one is happening at our zoo in two weeks. That's why we're trying to stop them now."

"Mom, did you look in this folder? Skyler was able to download pictures of all the arenas, as well as the clients' contact information, which VIP event they went to, and the animals they killed, many of which are close to extinction. She even downloaded some pictures of the hunters with their *trophies*."

"This is it, you guys. You did it!" proudly states Andrew, giving his son a fist pump.

"Are you serious?!" asks Avery. "We got them? For real?"

"Yes, you did," replies Lylyan. "They won't be able to deny that they're directly involved, nor that they're promoting the killing of endangered animals for profit."

"OMG! We did it!" exclaims Teagan.

"Wait up, guys," Skyler says. "Detective Williams, you should know that they found one of our cameras yesterday. I have a feeling you'll need to act fast—they've probably already started to cover their tracks."

CHAPTER 49

TEN DAYS LATER, Pike and Skyler make their way to Avery and Teagan's house to watch the evening news together.

"You're just in time," shouts Teagan through the living room window.

Avery opens the front door and jumps into Pike's arms, giving him a big hug. She quickly lets go. "Come in! It's about to start!"

Dumbfounded by this sudden burst of affection, Pike enters the house, speechless, with Skyler following in his footsteps, snickering at the site of cute puppy love.

Teagan gives everyone a bowl of popcorn and directs them to the basement.

"You made popcorn?" asks Skyler as they take the stairs. "You're a hoot!"

"I told her the whole thing will last only a few minutes," adds Avery, "but she insisted."

"Look! It's starting," shouts Teagan, grabbing a seat on the floor, less than a metre from the television screen. "Shh!" she mumbles, stuffing a fistful of popcorn in her mouth.

They watch in excitement as justice unfolds.

The reporter is standing beside the De La Grotta Zoo's main gates.

REPORTER: "Whaleford residents were stunned this morning when they found out that their cherished local zoo had been shut down after evidence came to light of serious animal abuse. Jill and Chris became members of the De La Grotta Zoo a few months after moving to Whaleford and have been coming every week for over ten years. Tell us, Jill, did you or your husband suspect anything?"

JILL: "We both had a feeling something was up, ever since the new owners took over, but we never would have guessed that they were killing animals. Why would anyone buy a zoo if it isn't for the love of animals?"

REPORTER: "And that's the question we've all been asking ourselves since the managing director of the De La Grotta Zoo was taken into custody last night. Mr. Donaldo Fleming is facing criminal charges for animal cruelty, killing endangered species, and illegally disposing of banned chemicals. More arrests are expected to be made in the coming days."

The reporter turns her attention to Pike's mother.

REPORTER: "Detective Williams, police forces around the world have been trying to arrest Mr. Fleming for years, but they've never been able to gather any incriminating evidence. How did you manage to crack the case?"

DETECTIVE WILLIAMS: "Well, a lot of the credit goes to a group of four remarkable young people. My son, Pike Williams, and his three friends, Skyler Matsui, Avery Westwater, and her little sister, Teagan Westwater. They managed to sneak into the De La Grotta Zoo and capture pictures and video footage. My husband and I were quite upset at first, as you can imagine, but without these four incredible teenagers, we wouldn't have been able to obtain warrants that led to these arrests."

REPORTER: "And that's not all. You convinced prosecutors worldwide to lay charges against every client featured in Mr. Fleming's international database."

DETECTIVE WILLIAMS: "That's right. All those who killed an endangered animal, in one of the hunting arenas, will be sentenced to one year in prison on top of paying a two hundred fifty thousand dollar fine, which will be distributed amongst the new zoo owners."

REPORTER: "Well, there you have it, folks. I hope this story helps to convince you that you're never too young to make a difference! Back to you in the studio, Tom."

CHAPTER 50

THAT NIGHT, Avery lies in bed, reflecting on recent events. She grabs her phone and searches for additional news coverage. She lands on a news article that features a photo of the four of them standing with the De La Grotta Zoo *welcome* sign. Teagan and Skyler are on the left, standing back to back with their arms crossed and huge smiles on their faces. On the other side of the sign, Pike and Avery look like a lovely young couple— with Pike's arm wrapped around Avery's shoulders and hers around his waist. This buzzworthy picture was taken earlier this morning when Detective Williams held the press conference to announce the arrests.

Avery texts the group chat, "Check out the pic I found online. We look great!"

"I love it! I just added it as my new background :)" replies Skyler.

Staring at the ceiling and smiling while thinking about all the animals they've rescued, she feels a warm, tingling sensation all over her body. She closes her eyes as each nerve ending resonates to a rhythmic frequency. She feels her inner consciousness gently slip into another dimension.

She walks toward a resplendent light that changes colour every few seconds—yellow to orange, to green and blue, to purple and pink—covering every spectrum of the colour wheel. Feeling the urge to look behind her, she turns and sees a tall, handsome being walking toward her.

"Pike!" She runs and jumps into his arms. They hug for a few seconds, feeling as though they are becoming one with the dazzling light. "Does this place look familiar to you?"

"Nope."

Looking at a distance, they are able to see—for the very first time—the entire alternate universe, and all the awoken protectors.

"*Whoa . . .*" they whisper in harmony.

There are a myriad of beings working together to safeguard Earth and its life forms. As they look beyond their own planet, they can see countless other beings doing the same for all life-sustaining planets.

"There must be millions of us stretching out across the universe. This is unbelievable," Avery whispers.

"The whole galaxy . . . no . . . the whole universe is connected. This is mind-blowing," Pike agrees.

"It sure is," says Zander, as he and Kamila appear.

At that very moment, the landscape morphs into a massive peninsula surrounded by several towering, boulder-type islands. The four of them find themselves standing near the edge of the highest island on a warm, sunlit, summer day. The air is filled with a salty, humid breeze brought on by each wave that drums the isle's rocky shore.

"Grandma," Avery cries happily. "It's so good to see you! And Zander! How are you?"

"I'm well, Avery. Kamila and I wanted to tell you both how proud we are of everything you achieved, and particularly without revealing that you are protectors."

"We can accomplish our true purpose by working with people who want to make a difference, but there's no reason to expose our powers," Pike replies.

"You're right. Sometimes, it's more effective to work in the shadows and help others realize they can make a difference," Kamila adds. "The four of you not only rescued countless animals, but you also helped raise awareness regarding the importance of shielding endangered species. In addition, you influenced the creation of an international community that will now collaborate to make the world a better place through their humane approach to managing zoological parks and wildlife refuges."

"When we started to awaken the protectors, our goal was to open the minds of millions of people—and it worked. Putting a stop to animal cruelty is only one of the phenomenal initiatives that protectors lead all over the globe ever since," Zander explains.

"Through this collective awakening, we've managed to slow down Earth's destruction," Kamila continues. "We are seeing the beginning of a significant shift for our planet and its inhabitants, but we still have much to do, and we need your help once again. This is why we have brought all of the protectors here tonight."

Avery scans her surroundings, taking in the thousands of colourfully-dressed beings sprawled across the peninsula—as though a child has dropped a bag of multicoloured jelly beans on a pebbled beach. "Why do I feel overjoyed and calm all at the same time?"

"Because you're surrounded by pure-hearted beings. If the protectors are successful, one day, all humans will feel the way you do right now—every moment of every day."

"That would be awesome," says Pike. "But how will we get there?"

"We have a plan—and we're almost ready to start. If all goes well, the awoken protectors will join forces, change the fate of our planet, and save the world, once and for all," Zander says earnestly.

"But hold on," Avery looks skeptical. "I don't want to be a downer, but there are close to eight billion people on our planet, and you're saying that a few thousand protectors are expected to save it?"

"That's right," replies Zander. "And the success of our mission lies heavily on the shoulders of human protectors."

"No pressure, Pike!" Avery raises her eyebrows.

"Pike and the other human protectors need to help humanity

understand that we are all interconnected—and that all human beings must act as upstanding global citizens. Once this is done, they will work to ensure only the brightest, most thoughtful, and respectful people become global leaders," says Zander.

"Seriously?" Avery looks incredulous. "That sounds impossible."

"Maybe, but I assure you, it isn't," replies Zander. "We're not expecting human protectors to accomplish this overnight. However, they have one thing going for them. The vast majority of today's youngest generations are fully aware that things must change—and change quickly. Human protectors will use their power of persuasion to entice them to take concrete actions that will actually change the planet's fate."

"That's awesome! I can't wait to start," exclaims Pike.

"And what about animal protectors?" asks Avery.

"Your group has been tasked to considerably reduce, and ideally eliminate, human consumption of meat," replies Kamila. "There are numerous negative environmental effects caused by meat production, including greenhouse gas emissions and deforestation, as well as land and water degradation."

"Seriously? I became a vegetarian because I felt bad for the animals, but I never knew that eating meat was harmful to the environment."

"It is," Zander continues. "There are billions of acres of agricultural land dedicated to growing crops to feed the animals that humans eat. These crops require enormous amounts of water and are constantly sprayed with chemicals, creating significant pollution worldwide. So, while the animal protectors are significantly reducing meat consumption, the water and the plant protectors will be rebuilding healthy ecosystems."

"We will reach out to water engineers to create eco-friendly, industrial-sized filtering systems to clean the oceans, rivers, and lakes," adds Kamila. "We will also help humans gain the required knowledge to build self-sustainable, artificial rain pods that will extract humidity from the air to create water that will be used to 'feed' some of the planet's driest areas."

"Are you saying that they'll be able to make it rain in the desert?" Pike asks in wonder.

"Exactly," replies Kamila.

"Whoa!" adds Avery, feeling awestruck.

"I know. Right? And once that's done," adds Zander, "we will bring about new species of vegetation that grow at unprecedented rates and don't require pesticides to flourish. We will also reach out to farmers to change their focus from raising livestock and cultivating fodder, to growing trees, plants, and vegetation to feed the world."

Pike happily adds, "That's so cool. All of our projects seem to be interrelated."

"They are," Kamila chimes in. "And that's why all awoken protectors must do their part."

"That's right," confirms Zander. "And there's still a lot more to cover. Once we start restoring the ecosystems, Avery and the other animal protectors will start working on the second part of their plan—reviving extinct species."

"How can we bring back animals that no longer exist?" questions Avery.

"Several decades ago," Zander continues, "when scientists realized the rapid pace at which we were destroying our planet and its species, they found a way to freeze the DNA of many animals that were close to extinction. Humans still don't have the scientific knowledge to do anything with the DNA, but we do. And when the time is right, animal protectors will share this knowledge to a select group of scientists who will be able to accomplish this mission."

"And these are just a few examples of the countless interconnected initiatives that are underway," adds Kamila.

"All of this sounds amazing, and I don't want to be a bummer," says Pike, "but people have been talking about the negative effects of human behaviour on our planet forever, and nothing's really changed. Why do you think things will be different now?"

"Because we will provide examples, as protectors, and show people that even the smallest act, the smallest change in their routine, makes a lasting difference. Especially if we have enough numbers on our side," replies Zander.

"And because we're finally at a point where most people realize the importance of following their heart and living their best life while supporting humankind and improving the world we live in," adds Kamila.

"They're right," says Avery. "If we can convince everyone to do their part, we will enable this generation to fix the mistakes of previous ones. If we all treat each other, and our surroundings, with respect, we can live on a peaceful and healthy planet."

CHAPTER 51

SEEING PIKE STANDING beside his bike, Avery pedals faster. Approaching, she shouts, "You're early! I should have guessed."

"We can't be late for the first day of school."

"You're such a *nerd*," she teasingly replies as she parks her bike next to his and sets up her lock. "So . . . any interesting dreams last night?" She winks.

"Actually . . . I dreamt I was an environmental engineer. We were married, had two kids, and lived happily ever after." He winks back, gently kissing the love of his life on the cheek.

They hold hands and walk through the school's main doors.

EPILOGUE

EAGERLY AWAITING THE CALL to start working on the guardians' overarching plan—and never wanting to feel as though they could have done more—Pike and Avery made a pact to follow their true purpose every single day.

A few days after the news report came out, Avery was offered a part-time job at the zoo. She spent the remainder of the summer working alongside Skyler and many of the previously fired staff who were thrilled to be asked to come back and revert the De La Grotta Zoo to a world-renowned animal sanctuary. On her days off, she enjoys spending quality time with her pets, and she never fails to save random creatures she haphazardly stumbles upon.

Pike and Teagan became the best of friends—spending many afternoons tucked in Pike's basement, building gadgets with Pike's father, who loves to encourage bright young minds to explore their scientific curiosity. Pike became a volunteer at a local retirement home, where he plays cards and checkers with the elderly twice a week. And he also took on the role of assistant soccer coach, where he gets to play with kids and help instill values such as honesty, fairness, and virtue.

Best friends . . . soulmates . . . however they choose to label their relationship, one thing is certain: Pike and Avery's inner beings are deeply intertwined—and will stay together—forever.

MAIN CHARACTERS

AVERY

PAIGE

JAKE

TEAGAN

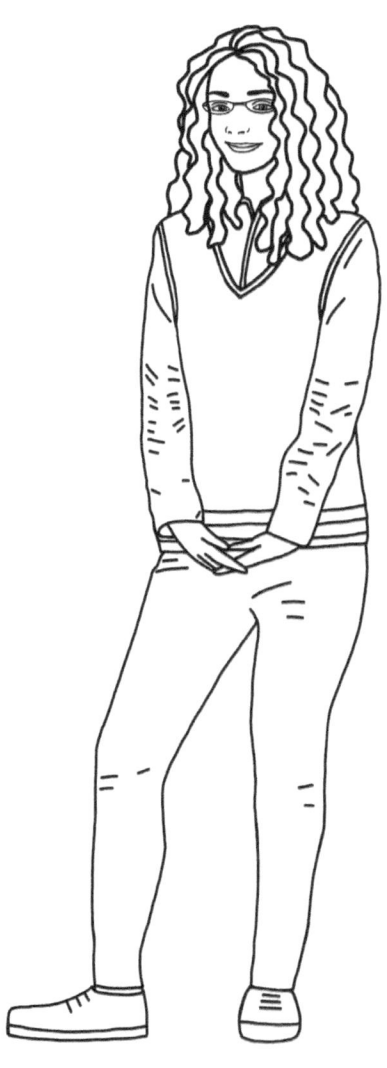

PIKE

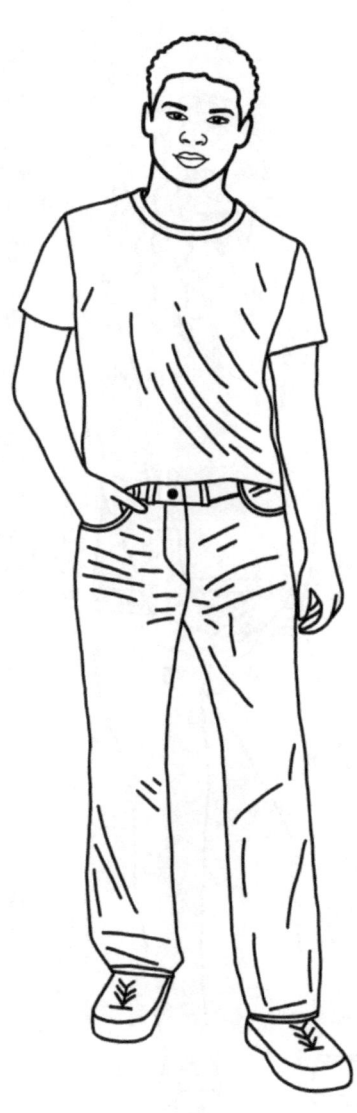

SKYLER

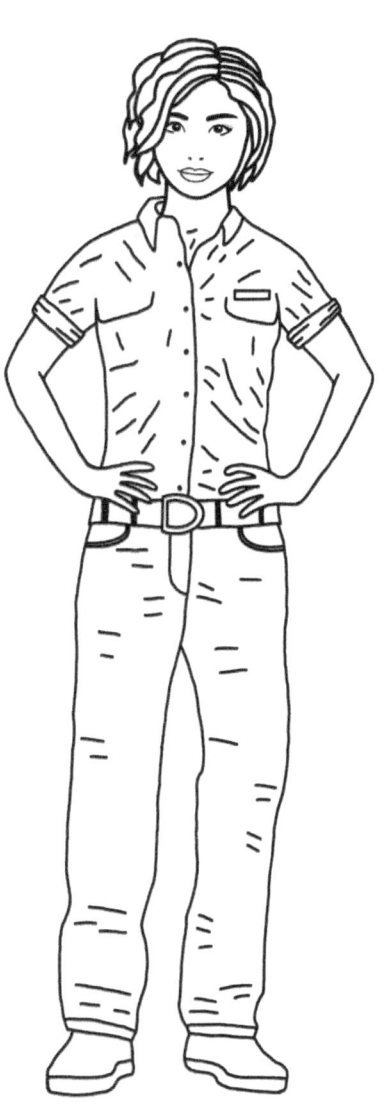

ZANDER

KAMILA

TATE

MADILYN

THEO

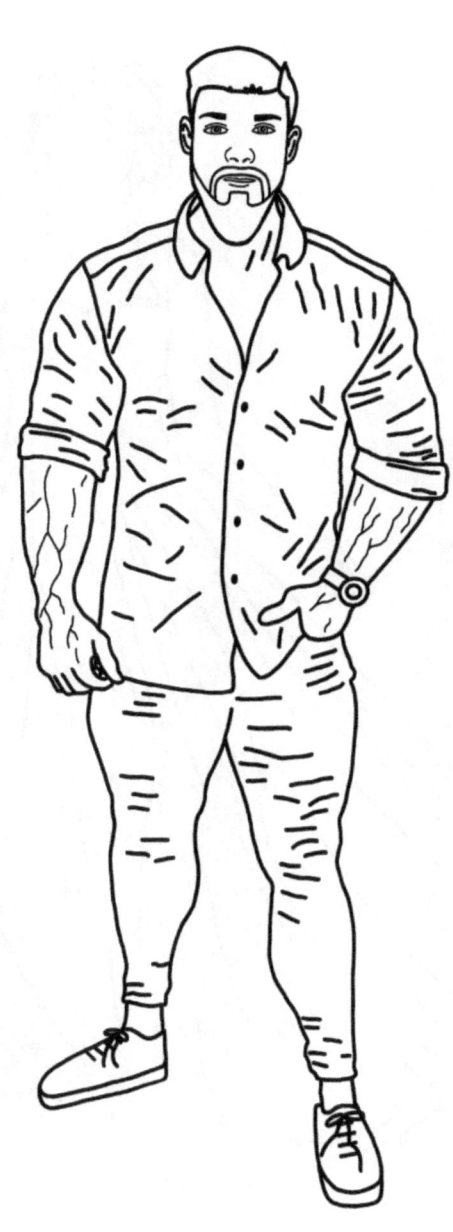

WILLOW

JASPER

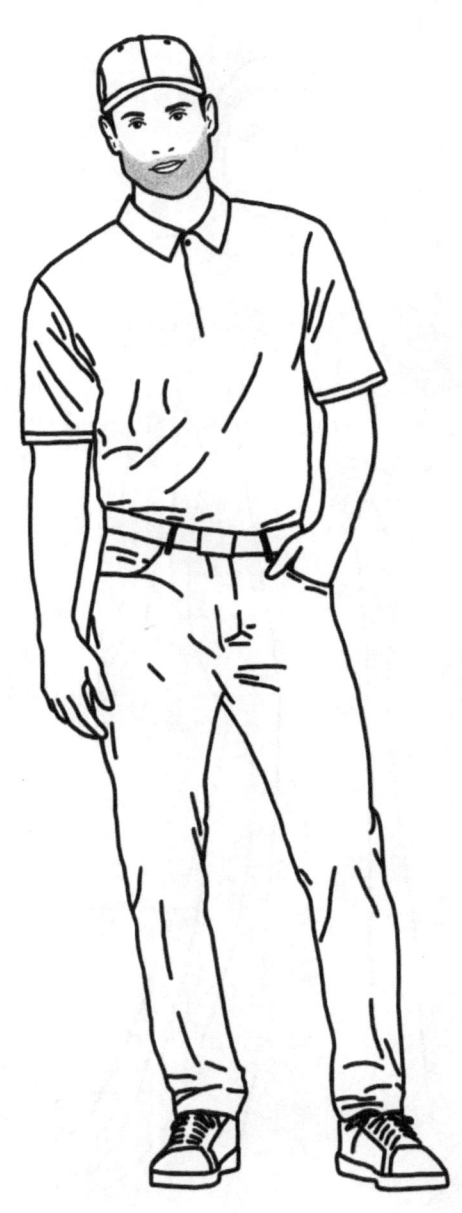